THE *MAGICAL* MAN LIST

THE *MAGICAL* MAN LIST

A Romantic Comedy About Finding Your Soul Mate

Christie Walker Bos

iUniverse, Inc.
New York Lincoln Shanghai

The *Magical* Man List
A Romantic Comedy About Finding Your Soul Mate

All Rights Reserved © 2003 by Christie Walker

No part of this book may be reproduced or transmitted in any form
or by any means, graphic, electronic, or mechanical, including photocopying,
recording, taping, or by any information storage retrieval system, without the written
permission of the publisher.

iUniverse, Inc.

For information address:
iUniverse, Inc.
2021 Pine Lake Road, Suite 100
Lincoln, NE 68512
www.iuniverse.com

Cover Credits:
Design: Robbie Bos

ISBN: 0-595-29239-9

Printed in the United States of America

Dedication

The Magical Man List is dedicated to those in search of their soul mates. Make a list. Create a ceremony. Let it happen. Everything you never knew you always wanted is out there. Making a list will help you recognize The One when he or she finally crosses your path.

Contents

THE *MAGICAL* MAN LIST

Chapter 1	The Game	3
Chapter 2	The Hospital	10
Chapter 3	The List	25
Chapter 4	The Ceremony	39
Chapter 5	The Wait	52
Chapter 6	The Man	67
Chapter 7	The Bar	77
Chapter 8	The Date	89
Chapter 9	The Test	101
Chapter 10	The Choice	114
Chapter 11	The One	130

Without Feeling Bonus Book 143

Acknowledgements

Thanks go to several key individuals who helped make this book a reality. First, to my very own 63-item man, Robbie—my soul mate, my inspiration, and my love—without whom there would have been nothing to write about. To my kids, Erica and Brian, for the hugs, love and encouragement along the way. To my family and friends, for their support in all my harebrained adventures and wacky undertakings. To my advance readers, Christine, Tina, and Angela, and to my copy editor, Julie, who made sure the words rang true and the dialogue was "real." To my agent, Rosalie Siegel, for her encouragement and care. To the folks at Dodger Stadium, for their assistance in "breaking in" to the Stadium, and to the folks at iUniverse, for making this book a reality.

The *Magical* Man List

CHAPTER 1

The Game

How was I ever going to find Mr. Right when I kept dating Mr. Wrong? I seem to have an uncanny ability of falling madly in love with the worst possible sort of men. I'm attracted to a nice package of external traits—mixed with a good sense of humor and a fun personality—plus several major flaws that I somehow overlook while trying to convince myself that *this* guy is The One. By thirty-five, my biological clock wasn't just ticking, it was starting the final countdown and I was beginning to have images of myself as the spinster aunt to my brother's kids. Panic was definitely setting in. Maybe it was because as I crept along toward the frightening age of forty, it was becoming increasingly more difficult to meet anyone at all—not to mention someone decent. My friend, Marta, was in the same depressing situation—both of us choosing unwisely over and over again. Of course, we could always see the flaws in each other's dates, but never our own. We needed help.

We needed something to help us make better choices. We needed something that would stop us from saying 'yes' to every decent-looking man who asked us out; something to help us be a little more discriminating; something that would short-circuit our flawed selection processes, bypass our initial urges, and help us find our soul mates. We needed a magical divining rod, and we needed it sooner than later. What we came up with was a combination of focused intention, excessive organization, dogged determination, and a sprinkling of magic—just for luck.

Our decision to get serious about finding our soul mates all started, surprisingly enough, from something that happened at one of our Wednesday night softball league games. On that particular evening, warm Santa Ana winds were creating dust devils around third base on yet another perfect Southern California summer night. The ballpark lights illuminated the infield and gave a soft glow to the outfield beyond. Small strands of my shoulder length, brown hair were whipping across my eyes, breaking my concentration and causing me to step out of the batter's box. The small crowd in the bleachers was clapping, adding to the excitement of the moment.

"Come on, Sam. You can do this," shouted my brother, Will, from his coaching position near third base.

I turned and gave him a thumbs-up sign and stepped back into the batter's box.

The summer of '95 was shaping up rather nicely, I thought to myself. Not only were the Dodgers—my favorite baseball team—on their way to a Western Division Championship, I had a big date right after the game with a genuinely nice guy I met through work. I had only known him for a couple weeks, but I was already thinking, 'This guy could be The One.' Then again, that's what I had thought about all my dates lately.

The older I got, the more pressure I put on each new dating encounter. When I was younger, I considered a date just something fun to do—maybe involving a free meal or a cheap feel—all of which were acceptable reasons for wasting an entire evening with someone. Now, every date carried so much weight; so much importance. From the moment a guy asked me out, I found myself leaping from one mental image to another, in a series of vignettes that highlighted our progressing relationship and culminated with me standing at the altar. All this happened even before I kissed the guy. I was hopeless. Sometimes I thought it would just be better to be single forever. There is nothing intrinsically wrong with being a never-been-married, single woman. It's just I had thought I'd be married and raising children by the time I was thirty. After all, in high school, I was voted "Most Likely to Get Married Before the Age of 21." It wasn't as if I wasn't trying to find my soul mate. I'd even had a few close calls, including a two-year engagement to a blonde surfer named Mike, when I was twenty-eight.

Everything had been absolutely perfect, right up until I caught him in bed with my neighbor's wife. I'll never forget that bitch's name. It was Nicole…something. Oh well, at least I'll never forget her face—or was that her bare ass that greeted me when I walked into my bedroom that day? It doesn't matter. She was butt-ugly any way you looked at her, which made the whole thing even more difficult to comprehend. The entire experience made me a wiser person for a whole six months.

Then I met Jonathan, the graphic artist, who liked to date—and sleep with—three women at once. Yuck. You would think I'd have figured out how to spot the "cheaters" by then—but apparently not. With no sisters to guide me through the nuances of relationships—only brothers—I was left to figure everything out by trial and error—one major error after another, that is. It wasn't as if my brothers, Marc and Will, didn't "try" to help me. Their helpful comments like, "Keep your knees together, and tongue in your mouth, and you'll be fine," or Marc's famous, "Guys only want one thing, so maybe you should consider becoming a nun," were an inspiration to me.

Besides scaring away potential dates, their biggest thrill was steering me away from their friends, knowing no good could come from a union of sister and friend. Either they would have lost their friend to me, or their friend would have done something stupid, like cheat on me, and they would have had to beat him up. I, of course, was always attracted to my brothers' friends and spent countless hours trying to insert myself into whatever they were doing.

That's how I came to love the game of baseball. It was the one sport they actually let me play, even if I was only allowed to stand in right field. Once I became good enough not to embarrass them too badly, my brothers actually let me play some of the infield positions—if they were short a player.

My only real dating guides, if you could call them that, were "the twins"—my inner voices. The twins are what most people might call their conscience—or their demons. I'm not psycho. Honest. Everyone has them. One little voice says, 'I wouldn't do that if I were you,' while the other whispers temptingly, 'Go ahead. It'll be fun.' I know I'm not the only person to have inner voices, but I am the only person I know who has given them names. I call one of them Goodie, short for Ms. Goodie Two Shoes, and the other one Lauper, for Cyndi Lauper's song, "Girls Just Want to Have Fun." I don't buy into the good versus evil thing, but think of it more as good sense versus having a good time.

The twins are never more outspoken than when I find myself in the middle of a really bad date. Sometimes they argue so loudly, I can't hear what the guy is trying to say. On my last really wretched date, the twins were in rare form.

I was on a date, courtesy of my dearest friend, Marta, who the night of our softball game was standing on second base, hands on hips, waiting for me to hit the ball. The guy was a civil engineer, like me, so Marta thought we would have plenty in common. "A perfect match" is what she had said. The evening started out okay; at least he had all the essential body parts, was taller than my five feet, eleven inches, and could carry on an intelligent conversation. But once we started talking about our work, he spent the entire evening one-upping everything I said. At first, I thought I'd be the humble woman and let him strut around a little and do the rooster-in-the-chicken-coop thing. But as the evening stretched on and on and on, he never tired of his role as proud cock. In fact, he embraced it, completely overriding, correcting or embellishing almost every comment I made. When he got up to use the restroom after dessert, the twins took over the conversation.

Can we go now? This guy is a jerk.
We can't just get up and go. That would be rude.
What? You don't think he's been rude? All he does is talk about himself and *his* great projects. It's as if our work is mere kindergarten doodles.
Oh, he hasn't been that bad, has he?
I think you were snoozing half-way through dinner. Not only is he an egotistical prick, he's boring, as well. If we leave now, we can be in a cab before he comes back.
We can't do that. That's mean.
Shit. Here he comes. Now we have to let him take us home. And since he bought us dinner, I'm sure he expects a good-night kiss—at the very least.
"Ugghhh," all three of us had groaned in unison.

Sometimes those two argue so loud, it's like bees buzzing around in my head. Every time I have another bad dating experience, I swear I'm going to give up dating forever. I tell myself that I'll just have to be happy being a single woman for the rest of my life because I just can't stand going out on one more disastrous date. My resolve usually lasts until a major holiday event or until I see one of those tear-inducing Hallmark commercials. The one that always gets me shows an older couple celebrating their fiftieth wedding anniversary. I sit there and cry and cry over this stupid commercial because I know I'll never have a cute, little, old man at my side when I'm old and gray. Certainly, not one who will buy me some sappy card that proclaims his love for the next fifty years. I always call Marta and she's crying, too—over the same sappy commercial—just like all the other single women in the entire state, the entire country—maybe even the entire world. After a good, long bout of self-pity, I find myself open again to the possibility of love, and accept a date with yet another misfit male.

While I was pondering my impending date, wondering if maybe, just maybe, this guy would be The One, the pitcher threw a perfect strike, which I let soar right over the middle of the plate, without even taking a swing. This elicited a burst of brotherly encouragement from Will.

"Come on, Sam! Choke up on the bat a little. You can do this," he shouted, as he clapped his hands together trying to bring some optimism to the moment.

It was the bottom of the ninth, bases loaded, with two outs, and unfortunately, I was at bat. The count was now two and two. The pitcher was on a roll—having just struck out the previous two batters ahead of me—and was looking to end the game with an easy out. [Our team was down three runs and would need a grand slam homer to win the game—something I'd never done in my entire existence on earth. Not that I hadn't dreamed of such a moment...even played it out in my head a dozen times. The play-by-play commentary came easily to mind.

"Samantha Stewart up to bat, bottom of the ninth with three men on. Stewart had a single in the second inning and a double in the fifth. She has the hot bat here tonight, folks, but will it be hot enough? Clark checks the runners, and then drills one in—95 miles per hour. Stewart watches it go by. Strike one. Next pitch comes in high and fast. Ball one. Clark stretches. Here's the pitch. It's a beauty, and Stewart can't resist. She gets a piece of it. Foul ball. Strike two. Runners lead off. Clark takes a quick look at first, then into his wind-up. Outside. Ball two. The crowd's getting anxious. They begin to chant–'Stewwwwart, Stewwwwart, Stewwwwart.' Stewart chokes up a little on the bat and steps into the batter's box. Clark adjusts his hat, checks the runners and goes into his stretch. He sends his heat straight down the middle, and "crack," Stewart sends the ball flying. It's going...going...it's gone! Grand slam home run for rookie Sam Stewart! The Dodgers win the pennant. The Dodgers win the pennant!"

But this wasn't the Dodgers, and I certainly wasn't going to be the one to hit a grand slam homer, and everyone knew it. My other brother, Marc, who was leading off third base, knew it; Marta, still on second, knew it; Carl, on first, knew it; both dugouts knew it; and even our loyal fans knew it. As a matter of fact, the outfield had moved up so close that they could carry on conversations with the infield. I really hated when they did that. On the rare occasion that I did knock one over the head of the second baseman, the centerfielder was right there, ready and waiting. It just didn't seem fair. If they would all just stay where they were supposed to be, like they do for the guy batters, I might have a chance.

My only hope was to hit a solid single and drive one runner in. That would take the pressure off me and put it on Mickey—the next batter—who was looking as resigned to the loss as everyone else. No, a single shouldn't be that hard to hit, especially in this league, I told myself as I choked up on the bat. My problem wasn't hitting the ball; my problem was running to first. Even if by some immaculate connection, I did manage to hit the ball over the centerfielder's head, I'd never make it home. I needed to hit a solid double just to guarantee I'd make it to first before the ball. Why? Because I'm a little slow. Okay, really slow. Okay, really, really slow—but it's not my fault, honest. In my junior year of high school, I had to have knee surgery after sliding into home and getting tangled up with the catcher. That pretty much ended my chances of playing softball in college and going on to be the first woman to play for the Los Angeles Dodgers.

So there it was. I was slow. And in order to hit a grand slam homer and have enough time to round the bases, I'd have to smack the ball well beyond the outfield boundary, into the parking lot, where it would need to roll under a truck and maybe even get stuck under a tire, just for good measure. But knowing all this, I still stood ready to make that game-ending swing, with my elbow high, eyes steady and the voice of the imaginary announcer filling my head saying, "Batter ready. Here's the pitch."

The pitcher, all cocky with confidence (the way most male pitchers get when they face a female batter), let a perfect pitch roll slowly off his fingertips. This ball was coming in so slow, so straight, with the sweetest little rotation that it was as if the entire world had turned into a made-for-TV movie, complete with my very own slow-motion sequence. Voices became muffled and garbled; a drop of perspiration traveled the length of my nose; my hands tightened their grip on the bat as my shoulders swung around and my hips swiveled to meet the ball. The "crack" the bat made when it connected with that perfect pitch was the sweetest, most satisfying sound I'd ever heard. It was exactly like I'd heard it a thousand times on TV, at the movies, and at Dodger Stadium. Just by the sound alone, you knew this ball was going out of the park.

No one moved, except the pitcher, as he watched in disbelief as his perfect pitch went sailing over his cocky little head. The base runners didn't move, the infield/outfield players didn't move, and I didn't move. We were all dumbfounded. Then, as if the slow-motion sequence had been sped up, voices became distinct again, and a single word rang out like a siren, repeated over and over: "RUN!"

I immediately dropped the bat, tossed off my batting helmet and took off running like a wounded dog. Marc crossed home plate well before I made it to first. Marta also made it home safely, and even Carl, with his well-developed beer gut managed to round third toward home. By then, I was exhausted. Running around all the bases—all in one play—was more running than I normally did in an entire game. I was afraid to see what had become of the ball, so I just kept my eyes on Will, who was frantically waving me in with wind milling arm signals.

I still like to relive that moment, with all the cheering and screaming coming from our dugout and our three loyal fans—Marc's wife, Bridget, Marc's daughter, Keri, and Freddie's girlfriend, Sue—all jumping up and down on the bleachers, screaming for me to run. I vividly recall thinking it was funny because I *was* running. As I approached home plate, I could tell by the catcher's stance that the throw was coming in. I could hear my brother screaming to slide, so with two steps to go, I went into a slide. Images of the slide that took out my knee flooded my mind, as I led with my good leg.

The next thing I knew, something slammed into my head. I vaguely remember hearing the sound of my brother's voice screaming, "She's safe!" and someone else, probably the umpire, shouting back, "She's out!"

Then, all of a sudden, everything started going dark. I felt as if I was being pulled into a dark tunnel. Even though I could swear my eyes were wide open, I could only see a pinprick of light. The shouting match continued. "She's safe. She's out. She's safe" Then, someone was shaking me and said, "No, I think she's really out…as in, out cold."

And then I was.

CHAPTER 2

The Hospital

The faint noise of a ballpark crowd was the first to break through the fog. Not the twenty-or-so people who normally attended our games, but the thousands of fans at a Dodger game—all cheering for something wonderful. My curiosity made me want to find out what was making the people cheer. Then I remembered *I* was playing in a game. I clearly recalled I was about to slide into home base and win the game. Was I safe? Did we win? Someone must know, I thought, so I struggled to open my eyes.

At first, I felt confused. I wasn't at the local baseball field, but rather in a room—a very ugly room with puke-green walls. I could hear the commentary of a baseball game coming from a TV somewhere. I tried to speak, but nothing came out. I tried again. This time, I squeaked out my question, which sounded something like, "Wuz I saaaafff?"

The next thing I knew, I heard my Mom scream, "Oh my God, she's awake," and then she started sobbing like a little kid, grabbing my hand like I had just come back from the dead or something. I still didn't understand what all the fuss was about. I could tell by the way the TV was mounted to the wall that I was in a hospital room—either that, or the world's ugliest motel room. Being the whiz kid that I am, I put two and two together and deduced I had been knocked out when I slid into home. A thought about the well-being of my body flashed across my mind. "Oh, God! I hope it's not my knee again," I thought. Slowly, I lifted my head to look at my prone form for signs of broken bones. Finding none, my mind returned to the game. I just had to know—was I safe or out? I tried again.

"Wuz I saffffe? Or Wuz I ouuuuut?" I croaked.

Just then, my Dad came into the room and immediately took my Mom into his arms. I think he started crying, too, which was really odd. Then he asked my Mom what I was saying. She started to laugh and cry at the same time, so her voice sounded even stranger than mine when she answered.

"After everything that's happened, the first thing she wants to know when she comes out of a coma is, 'Was I safe?' Not, where am I? Or, what happened? But was she safe? Can you believe it? She's still worried about that stupid game."

Coma? What coma? Who was in a coma? She couldn't be talking about me, could she? I felt fine. Just a little dry throat and strangely stiff all over, but a coma? Nawww, that's serious stuff. Maybe if I had a little water my throat would feel better and they would understand me more clearly. I tried to communicate again.

"Waaater. Can I get some waaater?"

Dad let go of Mom and came to me. He bent over the bed and kissed me on the forehead. I could see his hands trembling.

"Sure, princess, you can have some water," he said. "Let me just call the doctor to make sure it's okay."

Princess? Hmmmm. Dad hasn't called me Princess since I was twelve. Maybe I really was in a coma. Just then, Marc and Will came in and Mom started crying again as she relayed the good news. Will came over and punched me in the arm.

"I knew you'd make it," he said. "You're too stubborn to just go out the easy way."

Mom got mad at him for punching me, although he barely even touched me. Then Marc bent down and kissed me on the forehead and squeezed my hand. That's when I knew I must have been hurt pretty badly, because Marc would never kiss me like that—especially with witnesses around.

"Welcome back, slugger. You had us a little worried there," Marc said with a wide grin.

"You want to know what her first words were?" asked Mom, who was now in more control of her emotions. "She wanted to know if she was safe—you know, in that stupid softball game."

"Wow, you still remember that? That's great," said Marc while smiling at me.

"Soooooo?" I managed to say.

"Oh, you were safe, all right—very safe. You won the game for us, Sis. You hit a grand slam home run. With all the outfield pulled in so tight, you popped it right over their heads and that ball just kept rolling all the way to the parking lot. Your slide was perfect, too—right in under the tag. You would have been safe even if the ball hadn't hit you in the head. You were quite the hero," beamed Marc. "We went on to win the league championship, see?"

Marc was pointing to a huge softball trophy that sat on a little table next to my bed. Championship? How could they have already had playoffs? We were only half-way through the season. I was confused. Just then, the doctor (sporting a white coat and little tag that read Dr. Cho) came into the room.

"Look who's awake? It's our star patient. We thought you would be joining us sometime this week, especially with the World Series getting under way. Knew you wouldn't want to miss that," said Dr. Cho, winking at Marc, "even if the Dodgers didn't make it to the series again." He came around to the right side of the bed and took my hand to take my pulse. "Still strong as an ox, I see."

"She wants water," said Mom. "Can I give her some?"

"Not yet. But I'll have a nurse bring some ice chips. That ought to help her dry mouth."

Ice chips? I thought. Was I an invalid or something? Why couldn't I have a glass of water? So I started to sit up, but to my amazement, I couldn't.

"Samantha, what are you doing?" Mom scolded. "You can't just get up. You've been in a coma. You were hurt. Just lie still."

"How long?" I managed to ask, exhausted by my pathetic effort to sit up.

Everyone looked at each other, not willing to be the one to break the news. Dr. Cho finally stepped forward. Maybe he figured that's what he got paid for—giving people bad news. He cleared his throat and moved a little closer.

"First, let me ask you some questions. What is the last thing you remember?"

"I remember sliding into home, getting hit by something hard, and people arguing about whether I was safe or out," I said with a small touch of pride, still finding it difficult to talk.

"And what year is it?"

What year? Was this some sort of a joke?

"It's 1995, of course. I would think a smart doctor like yourself would know what year it is," I croaked sarcastically, wondering when I was going to get those ice chips.

"That's my sister—barely out of a coma and already cracking jokes," said Will, as he leaned his back against the wall.

"Yes, that was an easy one. Let's try something a little more difficult, shall we? What month is it?" asked the funny doctor.

"It's July something, I suppose," I said. As I spoke, I caught the looks on the faces of my family. Will was smirking, as if I had said something stupid. Mom and Dad looked sadly at each other, and Marc gave me a don't-look-at-me stare. How could I have the month wrong?

"That was a good try. Actually, it's October—October 20th, to be exact. You've been in a coma for a little over three months."

"Three months!" I blurted out, trying to sit up again.

The effort caused a major black-out and I was back asleep. This time, I merely fainted and was back in the world of the living within a few minutes—just in time to get yelled at by my Mother.

"Samantha Michelle, don't you do that again! You need to take it easy and regain your strength so we can take you home. There will be no more shouting and jerking about. Understand?"

Jesus! Barely out of a coma and already in trouble with my Mom. Typical. It doesn't matter if you are five, or thirty-five—your Mom is, and will always be, your Mom. So I just nodded my head and started to cry.

🍁　　🍁　　🍁

Three days after the "big awakening," as Marta liked to call it, I awoke to the tropical aroma of tuberoses and a huge vase full of soft yellow tulips. Tulips—my favorite flowers—don't smell like much of anything, so I always mix them with tuberoses. But only a few people know about my love for this strange flower combination: Marta, my brothers and my parents. Imagine my surprise when I discovered the flowers weren't from any of them. The card simply read, "Welcome back to the land of the living. I enjoyed being with you during your trip away."

Who could these be from? I thought. I figured it had to be either someone in my family or someone who worked at the hospital—maybe someone who took care of me while I was in comaland. I'd have to ask around to see if anyone knew who had sent the flowers. "Comaland" was the term Will invented to describe the period of time when I was out of it. Will would say things like, "While you were in comaland, I broke up with Wendy again." Or, "While you were visiting comaland, my roommate Seth crashed his car and almost joined you." It made it sound like I had gone to Disneyland or someplace fun and downplayed the seriousness of the situation. It caught on with not only my family, but with some of the hospital staff as well.

When Marta showed up that afternoon, she immediately zeroed in on the recent flower addition and the fact they were tulips and tuberoses, and went straight for the little white card.

"Enjoyed being with you during your trip—eh? Who are these from? Inquiring minds want to know."

"I have no clue. My guess is someone from the hospital or my family—someone who hung out with me when I was in comaland," I reasoned.

"Intriguing. Maybe it's some really cute, rich, young doctor, who fell madly in love with you," she suggested.

"Right. Maybe he came to my bedside everyday, under the pretext of taking my pulse, held my hand tenderly, and said sweet things like, 'I know you're going to make it, my sweet. You just have to. My life means nothing without you.'" I said with great dramatic flair.

Marta thought about that one, picturing the scene in her mind for a full ten seconds before reacting.

"Naw, it was probably some slimy guy from the cleaning crew who lifted your gown each night to check you out."

"Oh my God, that's disgusting," my body shook with revulsion at the thought of being scrutinized—not to mention, touched—by non-medical hands while lying helpless.

"It could happen."

"I know. That's what makes it so creepy. I like the doctor theory better."

"You know, I was here an awful lot when you were in comaland. I hate to break it to you, but there weren't a lot of cute young doctors running around. I think that's a TV thing. Most of the doctors I saw were between the ages of forty and sixty, and the only cute ones were married. I checked," she smiled.

"Thanks for looking out for me," I said sarcastically.

"I was looking out for you, and so was your family. I wish you could have seen them, Sam. It was an amazing thing to watch—your family in a crisis. Everyone was so there for you. If it had been me in that bed instead of you, I'd have been lucky if any of my brothers showed up."

Marta came from a typical family—meaning, it was totally screwed up. Marta's Mom had been a sweet, frail little thing who was terrified of her alcoholic husband. She rarely left the house, sending the boys to the store whenever they needed anything. Marta's father, on the other hand, was a not-so-quiet alcoholic who often burst into the house after an evening at the bar and turned it upside-down. Marta's brothers said it was like waiting for a hurricane to hit—knowing it was coming but never quite being prepared for the storm.

Being the only girl, Marta had been the apple of her Daddy's eye, even if that eye was often black and blue from some bar brawl. She still talks fondly about her Dad, although she realizes that if he'd lived much longer, she probably would have grown to hate him like her brothers did. Luckily, for the sake of the family, he died when Marta was barely ten, leaving her Mom and her five brothers to fend for themselves.

A few years after his death, her mother started acting strangely. On the rare occasion that she did leave home, she inevitably got lost and had to call one of the boys to come get her. It eventually got so bad that other people had to call the boys for her, since she couldn't remember that she even had children—let alone their phone numbers. In hindsight, it was obvious she suffered from Alzheimer's. But without another caring adult to interpret the signs, she just faded away, eventually dying when Marta was fourteen. Marta remembers her Mom as an aging Katherine Hepburn: beautiful, yet down to earth, and kind of flighty, like a wounded angel. Her favorite memory of her Mother was how she always sang Christmas songs all year 'round.

"They are such lovely songs," she would explain. "It seems a shame to only sing them at Christmastime."

Unlike my brothers, who derived great joy from torturing me on a near-daily basis, Marta's brothers were actually very protective of her. Her brothers watched over her all through high school, much to Marta's dismay, making it extremely difficult for her to get—and keep—a boyfriend. Because most guys would rather face one protective father than five older brothers when picking up a date. Consequently, Marta didn't date much.

"No matter what time I came to visit you," Marta continued, "someone from your family was here. And it wasn't just your immediate family. Some of your aunts and uncles came by—even friends and work people...it was amazing. Except for Sundays. That day was reserved for just your family. That's why when you woke up they were all here. They had all just come from church."

"It's so weird. All this stuff was going on and I don't remember a thing. I mean, what happened with my job? Do I even still have a job?"

"Your Dad took care of all that," Marta reassured me. "He paid the rent on your condo for the last three months and had all your utilities cancelled. I collected your mail and brought it to the hospital on Fridays. Your family took care of practically everything. Besides the mail, all I had to do was water your plants, which by the way, look much better now."

"Thanks. I can hardly wait to get home and out of this place. How is our little condo complex? All the same nuts and loons or did we get any interesting new arrivals?"

"The weird guy with all the finches in 507 moved out and was replaced by three eighteen-year olds who don't look old enough to drive."

"I'm glad that unit is closer to your place than mine. I'm sure they will be *great* tenants."

"Enough about boring stuff like bills and work. Tell me what it was like being in a coma," Marta said as she climbed on the bed with me, stretching out on her back and pulling an extra pillow under her head. She closed her eyes and pretended to be in a coma. "Was it just like being asleep? Did you have dreams? Or was there a white light at the end of a long, dark tunnel with your Grandmother calling your name…'Samantha, Samantha, come into the light'?"

"Nothing like that. There was the bonk in the head, a bunch of arguing, and the next thing I knew, I could hear a baseball game. When I opened my eyes, people started shouting and crying. It was no different than fainting, really,—except that I fainted for three months, not three minutes."

"That's kind of disappointing, if you know what I mean," sighed Marta. "I mean, where was all the cool stuff you see in the movies, like your life flashing before your eyes, or strange voices calling you forth? Even a real juicy dream would have been more interesting than this."

"Sorry to disappoint you. Next time I'll try to stay a little longer. Maybe you don't get to see the good stuff until you are in comaland for more than three months."

"No next time, please. I don't think your family is ready to go through *that* again."

Then she told me about my truly wonderful family. A physical therapist had advised my family to talk to me as if I could hear them, and to discuss everyday things—stuff I really liked. His theory was that people in comas could hear what was going on and the mental stimulation helped the recovery process. So my family took him at his word, and made sure someone was always here talking to me. They didn't come between ten p.m. and ten a.m. because, as Will so eloquently explained, 'even people in comas have to sleep.' Sometimes my Mom or Dad would spend the night on a small rollaway the nurses brought into the room each night. I guess they did that a lot the first month, but then the crummy bed started bothering my Dad's back, so they gave it up.

Each person had his or her own special routine. Marta said it was sometimes funny to walk in on it, because it seemed so normal, except for the part where I didn't talk back or respond to what people were doing or saying.

Mom often brought in old photo albums and retraced every family vacation, birthday party and Christmas over the past thirty-five years. She used the pictures to jar her memory and could talk for hours about the past: like the time we went to Yosemite and the bears ate our ice chest; or the time we all prayed for snow for Christmas, and ended up snowed-in at Lake Tahoe for three days. Marta said once when she came by, Mom was whispering, and tears were streaming down her face. The photo albums were laying open on my prone body, covering me like a patchwork quilt. When Marta came in, my Mom immediately wiped her tears and put on a big forced smile, motioning Marta to join her. She showed her the pictures of the family vacation when I broke my arm falling down a waterfall. I think comaland was much harder on my Mom than it was on me.

My Dad was into musical therapy. He would bring in a CD player along with his collection of country music. I hate country music, and he knows it, but Marta said every time he came, he put on a different CD and sang quietly to me. Marta thinks my Dad looks like a cross between John Wayne and Clint Eastwood, the older versions of both men. He is big like John Wayne, but has the weathered face of Clint Eastwood—and still looks good in blue jeans and a white T-shirt. If you want to see the Dirty Harry come out in him, just tell my mother to "shut up," then stand back and watch the transformation. With Dad, you could get away with all kinds of things, but if you made Mom cry, look out. He could make Dirty Harry look like a girlie girl.

I was told there was one song he played over and over, something about butterfly kisses, which made him cry like a baby. Marta said it was hard watching this huge man so obviously distraught.

Driving down the freeway months later, I actually heard that song on the radio. It sounded familiar, so I didn't turn to another station right away. Listening to the words, I could imagine my Dad sitting next to his comatose only daughter, and it even made me cry. I asked him later why he had chosen to play Country music when he knew I preferred Rock and Roll, Classical, New Wave—pretty much anything—anything, but Country.

"I saw it as an opportunity to brainwash you. I thought maybe when you woke up, you'd have all these songs stuck in your head without knowing why, and you'd suddenly take a liking to the stuff," he said proudly, happy that he'd thought of such a clever scheme.

But it didn't work. I still can't stand Country music. Marc told me the physical therapy guy had asked Dad if I was a Country Western fan. When Dad confessed that I actually hated the stuff, the guy laughed. He gently suggested that if Dad wanted me to come back, maybe he should play something that might entice me to come back. My Dad just said, "Oh," somewhat sheepishly, but the next day, he started playing some of my CDs. The funny thing was that his plan backfired and he ended up getting hooked on some of *my* music instead.

Marc, apparently, had his own daily routine. It revolved around our mutual love: baseball. Every day after work, Marc would arrive at the hospital with the sports section of the newspaper. He would take over for Mom, who went home to make dinner for Dad or take a break. Marc would sit next to me and start reading the sports section aloud, adding color commentary along the way. He once told me he had purposefully tried to rile me up by making disparaging comments about the Dodgers' pitching staff, even though they were our team. On nights when a game was on TV, we'd "watch" the game together. Marc would cheer and scream for the both of us. He spoke to me as if I could hear every word. People would pop their heads into the room, expecting to see a crowd, only to find my brother. Sometimes, he would bring both Bridget and Keri, and they would make it a family event. But normally, he came alone, right after work.

My niece, Keri, is so cute. She was a big hit with all the nurses, who kept bringing her things to play with every time she came to visit me. She's a precocious three-year-old with curly, strawberry-blonde hair and a sprinkling of freckles across the bridge of her tiny up-turned nose. Will and I give Marc a hard time because she has none of Marc's dark features, except for his dark brown eyes. Keri looks exactly like Bridget, who Marta thinks looks remarkably like Nicole Kidman.

In fact, Marta always describes people by comparing them to someone famous. She always asks, "What famous person does he look like?" I usually have a problem coming up with a match, except for when I'm called upon to describe Marta. She's easy—she looks like a tall Meg Ryan. She has neck-length white/blonde hair razor-cut with wisps of hair framing her face. She has clear blue eyes, a button nose and a perfect Meg Ryan smile. It's not just me; other people notice it, too.

Sometimes, strangers come up to her and ask if she's Meg Ryan's sister. The height thing always throws them, though. Marta is five feet eleven inches, a good three inches taller than Ms. Ryan. Marta's height is what makes her such an excellent first baseman—she has incredible reach. Marta can also be a little quirky, sort of like the character Meg played in *Addicted to Love*, a trait that only adds to the Meg Ryan-ish image. In more ways than one, Marta is a real Meg.

As for me, I don't think I look like anyone famous. While my dark brown hair is a standard feature for all the Stewart clan, my green eyes are uniquely mine. Mom, with her Mary Tyler Moore haircut, insists that my eye color comes from her side of the family, while my brothers point to my unusual eye color as proof that I was adopted. I'm tall, with an athletic build and breasts on the smaller size—a feature that has prompted much teasing from my brothers. My brothers gave me such a hard time growing up, in fact, I was surprised to hear about how devoted they were to me when I was in a coma. Maybe they like me better that way—silent and non-argumentative.

Will's visits were probably the most entertaining for the hospital staff. He played poker. He'd show up with a stack of chips, a note pad, and a deck of cards. Apparently, other people joined the game sometimes, but most of the time, because he had the late shift, it was just Will and me. According to eye-witness reports, Will would play for hours, playing both my hand and his. He would balance the chips on my chest, with the discard pile on my stomach, as if I were a card table. For once, having a flat chest had come in handy, he told me later. He propped my hand up in such a way that I actually held my own cards. The reason I can describe all this in such accurate detail is because I have photos. Will thought it looked so funny that he borrowed a friend's Polaroid camera and had the nurses snap some pictures. My favorite shows me holding a straight flush, a total set-up, and Will looking sad and depressed, as he chewed on a short cigar the hospital staff wouldn't let him light. He told me that occasionally, he smuggled in a beer or two, because he claimed it was too weird to be playing poker and NOT drinking beer. He didn't have a problem playing cards with a person in a coma, but playing poker without beer was, in his words, "just ridiculous." Only Will would think like that. One time, he even dribbled a tiny bit of beer on my lips, explaining that he didn't want me to feel left out.

He told me how much fun he'd had, and that I maintained the most incredible poker face he'd ever encountered. Right after that, he informed me that I owed him $10,000 in gambling debt, and I should really do something about my insidious addiction to poker.

Marta said there was always a parade of people coming in and out of my room—almost like a party. Everyone brought something, she said—flowers, food for my family (so they didn't have to eat in the café), and even a Kevin Costner Bull Durham movie poster to mask part of the puke green walls. I think one reason Will visited me so often was that he ate better in my room than he did at his bachelor apartment, where the standard fare was pizza or Chinese food.

"So, what did you do while you were here?" I asked Marta.

"I didn't come to see you very much. You were deadly dull and a horrible conversationalist."

"So you're saying I just lay here, not saying a thing, while you did all the talking? I don't see how that's any different than normal," I quipped.

"I came a few times, just to keep you honest. Someone had to make sure all this attention didn't go to your head. Besides, there were all the cute doctors that had to be looked after. I couldn't let you snag yourself a catch and leave me behind in singlesville alone," she explained as she got off my bed and started wandering around the room.

"I thought you said there weren't any young, cute doctors roaming the halls."

"No, I said all the cute ones were married. But how do you think I found that out? she said in a conspiratorial whisper. "Not all of the married ones wear rings, you know. I had to make inquiries, do some investigative work, and one-on-one interrogations. It wasn't easy, but I'd do anything for my friend."

"How can I ever thank you? So, you used the sympathy thing to try and score yourself a doctor, didn't you?"

Marta just shrugged her shoulders.

"You are truly pathetic. I'm in a coma, and you still manage to use me to break the ice for you. Did it work?"

"No. Like I said, all the cute ones are married. There was this one orderly, though, that caught my eye. We had dinner one night in the café. The food sucked, but the company was good. His name's Steve, and we've been dating for three weeks now."

Oh no. There it was—the three-week milestone. That meant, by my calculations, that poor Steve only had one more week before Marta started doing the goodbye thing, and Steve found himself discarded on the side of the road. Marta is the only person I know who is worse at the whole dating thing than I am. Something just happens, or in most cases, doesn't happen the way she thinks they should within that first month. When this "thing" does or doesn't happen, she just bails. No explanations. No second chances. She just bails. If having guy problems is the glue of female bonding, then Marta and I are stuck together for life.

I met Marta in college, in one of my junior year engineering classes. I was there because I actually liked engineering. Marta, on the other hand, was only there because she heard the guy-to-girl ratio was a least five to one. Although she was there specifically to meet guys, she took great care to never actually talk to, or sit next to, any of them. I quickly learned that this was my job: make initial contact, break the ice, and then if the water looked good, *she'd* jump right in.

The first day of class, she walked into the classroom, quickly surveyed the situation, spied me and another girl over to one side, and practically ran for the empty chair next to me. Marta was a hoot in class—always making the quiet quips and smart-ass remarks. They were always barely whispered, so no one ever heard them but me. By the end of the semester, we were spending more time with each other than with our respective boyfriends, so we decided to move out of the dorms and get an apartment together. Somehow, despite all the dating and partying, we both ended up with degrees and found decent jobs practically right after graduation. Marta's marketing degree and her outgoing personality landed her a job with the city of Santa Monica, preparing all their promotional materials and organizing their events. It's a great job, particularly because we get free tickets to all the local events. Marta found an older, but affordable, condo complex not too far from the beach in Santa Monica and moved in shortly after graduation. Two months later, another unit opened up for me, and we've been neighbors ever since.

Marta quickly became my relationship lifeboat and I became hers. She steers me through the treacherous waters of dating and faithfully throws me a life preserver whenever I have to abandon ship. In college, there were so many sunken relationships between the two of us, the body count surpassed that of the Titanic.

My first serious relationship was in college, with Stan, the ice cream man. We dated two whole months, which doesn't seem like long, but compared to the four-week trial period Marta gave her male suitors, it deemed us practically married. Stan was a fellow engineer and an excellent baseball player, so there were plenty of common interests. I had met him while playing a pick-up game at the park. When he struck me out in three—without any smirks or comments about my gender—I was intrigued. It wasn't until after we dated for three weeks that I learned of his strange addiction to ice cream. No matter where we were, or what we were doing, Stan needed ice cream every night at ten o'clock. It wasn't something one noticed at first. One had to be around him at the "witching" hour often enough to pick up on the pattern. After I spent one long weekend with him, his ice cream fetish became obvious. Each and every night, he had ice cream in some form or another—a cone here, a bowl there—even those ice cream nuggets at the movies. And it didn't matter what was going on at the time. The urge would strike and he'd stop everything—a movie, an argument, sex—anything to get some ice cream. In fact, Stan was so unique, he was the first guy to get one of our code names. We've used the technique ever since, to help us remember the ever-changing players in our personal line-ups.

There was Allen, "The Hand Guy," who only lasted three dates. I couldn't stand the way his hands flew around at light speed while he talked. I was actually afraid he might hit me while he was talking.

And who could forget the guy we nicknamed "The Skipper?" He liked phrases like, 'Ahoy mate!' and used a lot of boat jargon for a person who didn't own a boat. He was fun at parties, especially when a-few-too-many rum drinks impaired your judgment. Unfortunately, "The Skipper" was a lot of fun until you sobered up and realized he wasn't half as cute or fun as when you were both wasted. I didn't want to be cruel, so I dated him for two whole weeks before Marta pinched my cheeks, looked me straight in the eyes and said, "Why?" Since I had no good answer, I stopped seeing the infamous "Skipper" the very next day.

However, I wasn't the only one who had an affinity for picking the loons from the loony bin. Marta also had her share of wonderful dates and relationships. While my type of guy was usually the All-American, baseball-playing, athletic boy-toy, Marta preferred dark and mysterious, slick and fashionable, smooth-talking martini-pouring men. While I dated guys we nicknamed "Freckles," "The Skipper" and "Barney," Marta dated guys we called "Rico Suave," "The Shark," and "Hot Pants." The up side to our opposite taste in men was that we could walk into virtually any bar or club, and never find ourselves attracted to the same man. That's probably one reason we've stayed good friends for so long.

Before I decided to take a three-month vacation in comaland, Marta had been seeing a guy we affectionately called "The Snake." He received his nickname for his unique tongue-flicking style of kissing. Marta's description of his I'm-going-to-pleasure-you-tonight-woman tongue-flicking routine, could make me laugh so hard that I had to leave the room. It turns out "The Snake" couldn't handle taking a back seat to a woman in a coma. He stopped calling

Marta before she could stop calling him. So now, there's "The Orderly," Steve. At least, the poor, about-to-be-dumped Steve is making Marta smile *this* week. I was happy Marta had found Steve, just like I was happy each and every time Marta found The One. When my choices were as equally short-lived and random, who was I to say he wasn't?

Suddenly, all this talk about men and dating sparked something in my brain—something about a date. Oh, shit.

"Marta, I had a date scheduled for after that softball game, remember? His name was Drew. I met him at my building's little restaurant, The Lunch Box. Do you remember me telling you about him—tall, brown hair, blue eyes and a little shy?"

"Oh, yeah. I forgot all about that. Guess you stood him up, didn't you? Were you suppose to meet him somewhere or was he coming by the condo?"

"I don't even remember. What am I going to say if I see him again at The Lunch Box? He was such a nice guy and I was really looking forward to getting to know him better."

"I wouldn't worry too much. After three months, I'm sure he's probably written you off as a heartless bitch and won't give you the time of day next time he sees you. Then again, it could be just like that movie, *An Affair to Remember*, when Deborah Kerr is rushing to meet Cary Grant on the top of the Empire State Building, and gets hit by a car and doesn't show up."

"If I recall, Cary Grant was pretty pissed off for a long time," I reminded her as I tried to sit up straighter in bed.

"Yes, but it all turned out well in the end. After all, true love prevails," smiled Marta.

"Sorry, but the closest we are going to get to that happy ending is to rent the movie," I said, now a bit downtrodden.

"Cheer up. You're out of here in a couple days, and then we'll find you a real nice guy—or maybe even upgrade to a "man" this time."

"There are no nice men left in the world. I just stood up the very last one, and will never find another, ever again," I moaned, feeling pathetically sorry for myself.

I even started to cry and pulled the bed sheet up over my head in embarrassment. Just then, I heard footsteps enter the room.

"A little early for Halloween, isn't it?"

I pulled the sheet down and there stood Marc, with a bouquet of tuberoses and tulips. He immediately saw the other bouquet of flowers in the vase.

"Looks like I'm not the only one who knows your secret flower combo. Who are these from?" he asked as he walked over to read the card.

"A secret lover," I said sarcastically, while swiping the tears from my eyes.

"A secret lover, eh? They're probably from Will or Dad…or even Marta here."

"Don't look at me," Marta retorted. "I brought her the chocolates."

"Hey, I could have a secret lover," I retorted, sounding just as unsure as I felt.

No one responded, but both looked at me a little sadly.

"Come on. It could happen," I practically pleaded.

"Sure you could. We all could," said Marta in an attempt to cheer me up.

It didn't cheer me up at all, but did make me all the more curious about those damn flowers. I'd have to ask around. Maybe I really did have a secret admirer. Hey, it could happen.

CHAPTER 3

The List

I never did figure out who sent those flowers. Everyone in my family denied it, and no one at the hospital was talking. Three weeks after I got home, I was sitting alone in my living room, when it finally sank in—I had been in a coma; I could *still* be in that coma; I could have died. This was serious stuff. So I allowed myself to become very depressed. Not clinically depressed, mind you, where they give you Prozac or Zantax, which might have actually been fun—just the plain, old-fashioned variety of depression. I had experienced a near-death trauma, so I thought I earned the right to a little bout of self-loathing and emptiness. Marta and I called this the "hollow bunny" syndrome, when one feels all empty inside—kind of like a hollow chocolate Easter bunny, just waiting for someone to bite off an ear or two.

This was the second time in my life I had dodged the grim reaper. The first was a near-drowning when I was seventeen years old and obviously thought I was a much better swimmer than I actually was. I had to be rescued by a lifeguard in Malibu, which was pretty cool—until I ended up vomiting on his foot, which wasn't very cool. That experience changed my life for all of about a week. My close call with death gave me a new outlook on life, resulting in a kinder, gentler Sam who made a concentrated effort to be extremely nice to everyone she met. I was emotional over everything, to the point of balling over song lyrics that sung, "We may never pass this way again." This melancholy lasted about a week—just until some jerk cut me off on the 405 freeway. I instantly reverted back to my old self, flipping off the driver and making disparaging remarks about his lineage.

Yes, my epiphany didn't last long, but at seventeen what can one expect? I was young and had my entire life before me. Death was something that happened to "old" people—not teenagers—right?

But this time, it was different. I was no longer seventeen and fearless. Now I was a thirty-five-year-old, never-married engineer whose chances of finding true love, having some kids and living semi-happily ever after were looking bleaker with every passing baseball season. This brush with death had made me think this might indeed be it—the final inning, the last out. It wasn't so long ago that thirty-five was considered a long life. Of course, in those days, women also began bearing children at thirteen, which only heightened my sense of unfulfillment. My biological clock was still ticking. Only now, instead of being buried under a pile of sweaty softball T-shirts, that ticking time bomb sat on my nightstand, so it was the last thing I heard at night, and the first thing I heard each morning.

"Here's the problem," I explained to Marta, as we sat in the dry sauna at our condo complex. "I've always taken for granted that I would have children someday—a boy and a girl at the very least—and a wonderful husband. We'd live in a wonderful little house, with an office over the garage, where I would work from home, while raising my wonderful children."

Marta, who looked like a wise guru in her white towel turban and surrounded by a shroud of mist, simply nodded knowingly, while her eyes remained closed and sweat beaded up all over her naked body.

"But now I'm not so sure. My big plans depend, somewhat heavily, on finding that wonderful husband to father my wonderful kids and contribute at least something to the wonderful house," I said with an exasperated sigh. "Maybe this isn't all just going to fall into my lap like I thought, and maybe, just maybe, I have to do something more aggressive about it."

At this point, Marta opened one eye cautiously. She was in one of her down-on-men moods, after having dumped Steve, a.k.a. "The Orderly" less than a week ago.

"What can you do about it that you haven't already been doing? I mean, you're still dating. You're still 'out there' on a regular basis, just like me, and look what it's gotten us so far—an assorted collection of anal retentive freaks and losers."

"I know. That's why I'm so depressed. I'm in a rut and don't know how to get out of it. I'm running out of ideas. It's time to take this finding-a-life-partner stuff more seriously. It's the bottom of the ninth with two outs."

"Please, no baseball analogies," Marta pleaded. "We have a problem and this time we need something a little stronger, a little more mystical, a little more magical than baseball."

"You blasphemer," I cried in mock horror. "What could be more powerful than the sacred game of baseball?"

Marta sat silently for a moment, pondering over our dilemma. Finally, she started speaking very slowly as if each thought had to be pulled from deep inside her head.

"What we need is something to guide us in our dating choices. Something to help us choose more wisely, instead of being swept up in the moment. Maybe even some kind of magical dating formula. Maybe we need to make a list," she said, sounding very profound. "I keep hearing about this list thing. It's really supposed to work."

"A list? What kind of list?" I asked, waking the twins out of their stupor.

"A magical, spiritual wish list that will bring your soul mate to you," said Marta, now sounding like the guru she resembled, except for the naked part, that is. I think most gurus wear a white diaper or something. It was hard taking Marta serious while she was naked.

"Haven't you heard it at least a dozen times? If you want to succeed, if you want to get ahead, make a list of your goals. If you want to feel organized and in control of your life, make a list of projects, errands—even a small to-do list will work. And when you've crossed everything off the list, you gain a wonderful feeling of accomplishment and satisfaction."

"How does this get us a man?" I wanted to know.

Marta explained her theory of why the list thing might work for us.

"Creating a list forces you to really examine what it is you really want, and writing it down makes it tangible and real. The list then becomes a form of meditation, or prayer—a concentration of personal energy that draws the right person to you. Maybe we could empower our lists with magical forces by creating a sacred ceremony or something."

Ms. Goodie was instantly suspicious.

This will never work. Sounds like a bunch of New Age mumbo jumbo to me.

Oh shut up. Let's find out more before we pass judgment, shall we?

"So we're going to make a wish list for the perfect man? I do that every Christmas and it hasn't worked yet."

"I've seen your Christmas list posted on your parents' refrigerator. It's a joke!" laughed Marta.

And indeed it was. Every Christmas, since I turned twenty-one and became too old for a real Christmas list, I created a joke list that went up on my parents' refrigerator every Thanksgiving. I asked for things like a million dollars, world peace, a Jeep complete with golden retriever, a condo at the beach, and a man. At first it just read, "A man" but as the years went by, I kept elaborating—a man with a job; a man who didn't live with roommates named The Bomb and Six-Pack Man; a man with a brain above his neck; a man who remembered your name the next morning; a man who didn't sleep with your girlfriends; a man who could chew gum with his mouth closed and not swagger at the same time; a man who was taller than he was wide. Simple requirements, really, but come Christmas morning…nothing. One year, just as a joke, Will decided to grant my wish. He had stuffed a fully-inflated man into an empty television box and when I opened the gift, knowing full well it wasn't the color TV pictured on the box, I screamed as the anatomically correct plastic man-doll came springing out.

"So what kind of list do you have in mind?" I asked, only slightly intrigued.

"I'm talking about a fool-proof, everything-you-want-in-a-man/soul mate, type of list, complete with magical powers, a special spiritual ceremony and summoning chant."

"I think we'd better get you out of here. All this heat is causing your brain to swell. You might even be having a stroke."

Leave it to Marta to turn a simple thing like making a list into a spiritual event. Once, when both our boyfriends had dumped us within a week of each other, Marta decided we needed a cleansing ceremony. We took a bottle of wine and some of the boys' personal possessions to the fire pit at the condo. After starting a nice little bonfire, we had to abandon the ritual when the dirty gym socks produced a most rancid stink.

"Okay, let me put it another way—a way that you'll get. 'If you build it, he will come,'" she said, trying to sound all mysterious and other-worldly.

Immediately, images of Kevin Costner plowing under his corn and turning it into a baseball field, came to mind. If you build it, he will come. The words floated around the sauna on waves of rising heat. The more I said it to myself, the more I began to wonder if it just might work. Hey, if it worked for Kevin, why not for Marta and I?

I can't believe you are buying into this shit.
I kind of like it.
You two are hopeless.

"All right, I'm intrigued," I said, trying not to sound too interested. "I might consider doing this, but only if you do it, too, and as long as we don't tell another soul—especially not my brothers. I don't want anyone thinking I'm some kind of pathetic freak that has to rely on some magical wish list to find a man."

"They already think you're a freak. After all, you're almost forty and still single. How freaky is that?"

With that, I pulled the towel off my head and gave her a good snap on the thigh.

Thanksgiving was right around the corner, and I couldn't get Marta's idea out of my head. If I build it, he will come. Maybe Kevin Costner wasn't the only one who could build a dream, make a little magic happen. If I created a list—a very specific list of what I wanted in the perfect man, the perfect man for *me*—then it would be easier to find such a person. Instead of walking into the "man store" and picking out exactly what I wanted, I had been wandering aimlessly up and down the aisles, trying a little bit of this, sampling a little bit of that, discovering what I didn't like more than what I did. With all the poor choices I'd made, I should know by now what I want, what I really want. And so, one week before Thanksgiving, I called Marta.

"Okay, you convinced me. I'm going to do it," I said, sounding way more confident than I felt.

"Do what?" she asked, drawing a complete blank on our conversation in the sauna.

"Make the all-great-and-powerful list, remember? You said I needed to make a list to help me find my soul mate."

"And you're actually going to do it?" she said, sounding skeptical.

"Yes, and so are you!"

And that's how we ended up in the community hot tub at our condo complex, at ten o'clock at night on the Saturday before Thanksgiving. It was a great night for creating magic. The community hot tub was tucked away in a corner of the pool area and surrounded on three sides by tall banana palms. A cool ocean breeze was lightly blowing the leaves keeping the sky clear. You couldn't see any stars, but then again, you rarely could around here. There was, however, a half moon giving us just enough light to write our lists by. With one bottle of wine, two pads of paper, two pens, and the future of our love lives held tentatively in our prune-like fingers, we prepared to create a wish list for two perfect men.

"So where do I start?" I asked, holding pen and notepad slightly above water level.

"I think you should start with items you can easily determine within the first five minutes, then move onto things you may be able to tell after an evening together, then onto stuff that might take you a month of dating to discover, and finally, get to things you can only discover in the bedroom," finished Marta with a smile.

"Well, that will never work for you. You end up in the sack within the first week."

Marta gave me her version of a rotten smirk and then ignored me. After taking a large gulp of wine, I focused on the task of creating my list. First, I started with the physical stuff, knowing those items could be ascertained as soon as you meet a guy. I called this group of items the top ten, but not necessarily the most important ten items. Most of what one can discover in the first ten minutes is pretty superficial. But by putting these traits first, I would be able to eliminate a lot of people before they even opened their mouths. I know this sounds rude, but everyone does it. It's called having a type—the basic requirements that attract you in the first place. I tried to keep my top ten pretty general, so as not to eliminate a potential soul mate on insignificant details.

"So what's your type?" Marta wanted to know.

"He absolutely has to be at least my height, but preferably a couple inches taller."

At five feet, eleven inches, I'd dated my share of shorter guys. I have nothing against short men, in general. Several of my dearest friends are short fellows, I thought.

"Dating shorter guys always makes me feel like an Amazon woman—like I have to protect and care for him. I hate feeling like that, don't you?"

"That doesn't bother me. What if the guy is simply gorgeous, but just a few inches shorter than you—will you refuse to date him?"

"Are you going to question my every line item, because if you are, we're going to be here all night."

"Fine. I just thought you'd appreciate my input. Continue on. He has to be tall…"

Tall is important and, luckily, easy to measure. Next, I eliminated extreme body types. I didn't want someone who was overly fat—or super skinny, for that matter—so I put down "an athletic build, but not a hard-body." I wanted to be realistic. To require a perfect human form, I thought was asking a bit much, especially when I'm far from perfect myself. Besides, the guys with the perfect bodies usually turn out to be either gay, or so obsessed with their own good looks, they spend way too much time in the gym. I wanted this guy to love *my* body not his.

The age thing came next. Having dated the full range, from ten years younger to twenty years older, I definitely wanted someone closer to my own age this time. I put down a maximum of five years younger or ten years older, although I was pretty sure I'd fudge on this point if the perfect man was a few years off in either direction.

When it came to eyes, having two of them would be a good start, but the color wasn't a critical factor. Alive eyes that have a twinkle is what turns me on. I wanted eyes that looked into my soul and made me feel like I was the only person on the planet. This has more to do with how a person looks at you than about the eyes themselves.

Some women are big on lips—yummy, kissable lips. I know Marta is. But I didn't put that on my list. I don't really care what they look like as long as he knows how to put them to good use. I'm also not real particular about facial hair or hair length either, although a guy who has longer, thicker, or more beautiful hair than me might be annoying. Personally, I think it's the woman who should wear the hair in the family. So to my list I added a very vague 'nice hair.' Almost as an afterthought, I added that the perfect man had to be in good health. I didn't want my soul mate to die suddenly from some horrid disease. I'd leave that scenario for one of Eric Segal's tragic love stories. I wanted a happy ending. I recapped my list so far for Marta, who didn't seem to be doing much writing of her own.

"That takes care of the first five minutes," said Marta as she took a sip of her wine. "So you've seen this guy, he looks good, now what?"

"Physical attraction—him for me and me for him. A spark. That little lightning bolt that zings across a crowded room, hits you between the legs, and makes you say, 'Ohhhhhhhhhhhh. Who's that?'"

Marta sighed. "I just love when that happens."

"But beside the physical zing, I want the spiritual Zing as well—the feeling that this person fills up your heart like a song, and gives you a happy heart."

"I agree; that's a must. Then what?"

I wanted someone who could carry on a decent conversation, someone who wasn't totally clueless about current events, history and common stuff. I didn't want a brainiack, either. I had no interest in being with someone who tries to impress me with everything he knows. I get extremely bored listening to those people—men and women alike. So I wrote down, "good conversationalist," but then added "but not too good." This may have seemed strange to others, but I knew what I meant. Next on the "hit list" for Mr. Perfect was a note about being financially self-sufficient. I wasn't interested in anyone who was still living with his parents, unless he had invited them into his home instead of placing them in a nursing home—a decision that I would consider sweet.

While having a job and being self-sufficient were important, being rich was not. Money doesn't impress me, so I didn't put 'he needs to be rich' on the list. I simply didn't want to support him. And while I was on the subject of jobs, I noted that he should love his job. It didn't matter to me what he did for a living, as long as he loved it and felt fulfilled by it. If he was the school handyman, I didn't care—as long as he *loved* being the school handyman. I'd already spent far too many nights stuck on a barstool, listening to some forty-year-old man talk about how he hated his job, hated his wife, and hated his life. My soul mate needed to have a zest for life, love his job and be an all-around happy person. I wanted him to be in touch with his inner child and not jaded by life. This, in itself, would eliminate most of the thirty-eight to forty-three-year-olds I currently knew. I wanted someone who wasn't too serious about himself or life; someone who had his ego in check; someone who could laugh at adversity; and someone with a good sense of humor.

"Don't you think a good sense of humor is an absolute must?" I asked, as I jotted down my previous ideas and struggled to keep the paper from getting wet.

"Good sense of humor? Sure, but everyone says that. Why not try being a little more original?"

"Everyone says it because it's an important quality. I want to laugh with this person. When we go to a movie, I want him to laugh at the same things I'm laughing at, I want him to get it. Maybe I should clarify the statement by saying he should enjoy the same type of humor as me. I'm not really big on sarcastic, cutting humor, especially when the cuts and jabs are directed at me," I said, thinking of a particular witty young man who turned out to be quite vicious.

"What about me? I can be sarcastic, and you still like me," said Marta making a pouty face.

"First of all, I don't want to marry you and spend the rest of my life with you. And second of all, who told you I liked you?"

At that, Marta squirted water at my face with her cupped hands.

"Hey, you're getting The List wet!"

"Doesn't matter. You'll have to rewrite it on nice paper anyway. Speaking of movies, I think you should put something in there about his taste in films. What if he likes nothing but *Kung Fu* films or *Rambo 1, 2 and 3*? We can't put up with that!"

"We? I thought this guy was for me?"

"I was thinking of my List," confessed Marta.

"Speaking of your List, why aren't you writing?"

"We'll do my List another night. I'm just jotting down good ideas we come up with so I can add them to my List. I think the movie thing is a good one."

I agreed, so we started making a list within the List of all our favorite movies. We thought he should count among his favorites at least some of the following: *Blazing Saddles, Last of the Mohicans, The Princess Bride, Sleepless in Seattle, Big, Young Frankenstein*, all the *Star Wars* films, *Monty Python's Search for the Holy Grail*, and *A River Runs Through It*. Then there were the baseball flicks: *Bull Durham, Field of Dreams* and *A League of Their Own*. This was critical to relational success because lines from our favorite movies have invaded our lives, and become a part of our everyday vocabulary. I wanted the person I was with to get it, when I quoted lines from *Young Frankenstein* like, "Put zee candle bick," or, "Walk this way," as I limped off, dragging my bad leg behind me. Or, when I hit my chest and announced in a deep voice, "Good trade," like in *Dances with Wolves*, or declared, "Someone needs to go back to town and get a shit-load of dimes," like in *Blazing Saddles*, or say sweetly, "As you wish," like Farm Boy in *The Princess Bride*. Marta and I can do movie lines for hours. I simply couldn't imagine spending the rest of my life with someone who gave me a blank stare every time I rattled off a favorite movie line.

"Just once in my life, I'd like for someone special to look me in the eyes and say, 'Stay alive, no matter what occurs. I will find you, just stay alive,' with all the passion and fervor of Daniel Day-Lewis in *Last of the Mohicans*. If that ever happened, I think I would actually swoon."

"Well, then put it on your List. It could happen," Marta said, in her best Long Island accent.

So that went on The List, "Wanted: Man who appreciates a well-timed movie line, and knows the ones I'm quoting without having to ask." This is never going to happen, I thought. I'm being way too specific. But Marta insisted this had been my problem all along, I hadn't been specific enough—I hadn't been focused. She said I needed at least fifty items on my List to make it work. Fifty items seemed impossibly picky.

So now I've met this person—he's tall; he's healthy and fit; he makes me laugh; we have the chemistry-thing going for us; he gets my movie quotes; he's happy; he has a job he likes; and he's fun to be with. So far, so good. We go out on a few dates, and that's when it usually starts to fall apart. I inevitably start finding the little things that I don't like—or not necessarily that I don't like, but things I wished he would do and doesn't, like hold my hand in public, or be more romantic. So I added that he must be physically affectionate. He needs to enjoy touching and being touched. I wanted him to enjoy giving massages as much as receiving them. He also had to be a good kisser, and have incredible passion—for both life and me.

"I'm well over twenty items already. What else should I put down?" I asked, taking a break to refill my wine glass.

"Back up a minute. What do you mean by 'good kisser?' I think you need to be more specific," Marta prodded.

"It's something you just know when you're doing it. But, if I had to describe it…"

"You must, you must."

"I'd say his kisses should make me melt—starting with my lips, moving down my throat, tickling my breasts like a soft summer breeze, and finally making my legs feel like I can't support my own weight. I think Kevin Costner described it perfectly in *Bull Durham*…"

"I believe in long, slow, deep, soft, wet kisses that last three days," both of us said dreamily, in perfect unison.

"Now that was a man," sighed Marta. "And what a sex scene. I love the way he swept the kitchen counter clean, so they could do it on the counter. I'm putting that on my List—someone who can be dramatic."

"I loved it when they made love in the bathtub and the water sloshed all over the place and put out all the candles. What symbolism! Ever since I first saw that movie, I've wanted to buy a bathtub like that."

"I would buy one, too—especially if it came with Kevin Costner," laughed Marta, giggling like a five-year-old. "Speaking of sex…When do you put the sexual requirements on your List?"

"I have to put those in writing?"

"Of course! You don't want to find the perfect man, only to find out he's lousy in the sack. Oh, and that reminds me, add 'single or divorced' to your list, just as a precaution. You don't want Mr. Right to be someone else's Mr. Right."

"Not married or involved. How's that?" I asked, and got a nod of approval. "I think I'll add my sexual requirements later, in private. For now, I'll just put a vague, 'good in the sack.'"

"You're no fun," complained Marta.

At first, I thought coming up with fifty to sixty items was going to be difficult. But the more we talked, the more ideas we came up with—and we hadn't even finished the first bottle of wine, yet. We moved on to similar interests. Number one on the List was, of course, baseball. The guy had to have an appreciation for the game. If he didn't actually play himself, he had to be willing to let me play, and even come to my games occasionally. I'd be damned if I would marry a guy who told me I couldn't play in my Wednesday-night league. It would be a bonus if he was a Dodgers fan, but that wasn't a requirement. It would be all right if he liked the Angels, the Giants, or even the Padres…although, who would like the Padres? If he was a Cubs or Yankees fan, however, I don't think I could stand it. So liking baseball was a must. After that, I was pretty much open. He should also like outdoor activities, such as hiking, biking, fishing, skiing, boating and camping, but couldn't be fanatical about any one thing to the exclusion of everything else. His taste in music could be anything but—you guessed it—Country. And he'd get bonus points if he loved Jimmy Buffett as much as Marta and I did.

Marta and I have been Parrotheads since we went to our first Buffett concert in San Diego. A Parrothead is the equivalent of a Deadhead only with a Caribbean twist. Each year, hundreds of thousands of crazy Parrotheads gather at Buffett concerts dressed in various combinations of beach wear, Hawaiian clothing and Caribbean soul outfits to drink margaritas in Margaritaville, eat Cheeseburgers in Paradise, and sing along to Buffett songs at the tops of their lungs. It's become an annual tradition for us to load up the car with beer, tequila, beach chairs, grass shirts, stuffed parrots, and a Buffett buffet, and head to the parking lot for the craziest tailgate party on the planet.

"Wouldn't it be great if my soul mate was a Parrothead?"

"Sure. If he's not, he must be amenable to conversion. But what's this you mentioned about bonus points?"

"Bonus point items aren't deal breakers. Imagine if the perfect guy met all my criteria and played baseball in the major leagues, or had great season tickets, or a sexy Australian accent, or actually knew Jimmy Buffet and could get us backstage passes. That would be bonus points."

"Dream on, girlfriend. But I'm proud of you for thinking big. What would your deal breakers be? I think you should list those, as well. Kind of the 'thou shalt not' side of the List—such as 'thou shalt not be an ax murderer or wife beater.'"

Coming up with the list of "shalt nots" was actually pretty easy. We just considered every past boyfriend we ever had, and the list practically wrote itself. According to my list, my soul mate "shalt not" be an alcoholic, drug user, wife beater, felon, child molester or control freak. Neither could he be a game player or liar. Add to that an undependable, two-timing scumbag, who sleeps with other women when he's only supposed to be sleeping with me. That about covered it. And Marta seemed satisfied.

"I think you're safe now. How about all the emotional, hard-to-define qualities, like patience, displaying kindness to animals and small children, exhibiting a sound moral character and religious beliefs—stuff like that?" she asked, taking another sip of wine and topping off our glasses.

"I'm sure my Mom would want him to be Catholic, but I really don't care. I'm more of a cafeteria Catholic, and lately, not even that. When it comes to religion, as long as he doesn't try to ram his beliefs down my throat, he can believe—or not believe—whatever he wants. But he has to be a kind and honest person."

"This guy is sounding better and better," teased Marta. "I might even be interested in this one."

"You're supposed to be creating your own List, not copying mine."

"At this point, I'm more interested in your List than mine. What else should we add?"

The family-thing was the next area we tackled. We both agreed that getting along with my brothers, and respecting my parents, was a priority. I also thought it was important that his family liked me, at the very least, and better yet, loved me. Then there was the whole issue of kids. I wanted to have at least two children, and if he was dead-set against having children, we would have a problem. If he already had kids of his own, I would still want to have at least one together. After all, it would be a shame not to pass on the genes of two such perfect people! Getting together with friends and family is also important to me, so I scribbled down something about him not being a loner or recluse.

"And he absolutely, positively, has to adore you, Marta," I said, as I wrote and underlined 'Must like Marta.'

"Here, here. I'll drink to that," she said, finishing off the last of the wine. "Anyone who doesn't adore me can't possibly be a decent human being, can they?"

"True, true," I agreed.

"I'm getting tired. Are you almost done? You must have at least fifty things by now, and we're out of wine," said Marta, yawning.

"Except for the sex stuff, I think my list is done. Let's see, I have fifty-seven requirements, not counting bonus points. That should be more than enough, don't you think?"

"You've made a great start," she agreed. "You can always add to it later, as you think of other things. Now let's get to the interesting stuff—sexual preferences. Go ahead, I'm ready to take notes."

"I thought I was going to do these in private?" I protested, perhaps a bit too loudly.

"And deny me the pleasure of the cherry on top? I don't think so. Besides, you end up telling me absolutely everything about each and every one of your lovemaking sessions anyway, so what's the difference if I know now as opposed to later?"

"I guess you're right."

I started thinking about what really mattered in the sexual arena. Most importantly, he should think I'm sexy. Looking at me should turn him on something fierce, because that turns me on. When he sees a hint of breast in my low-cut dress, or my nipples showing through a little tank top, it should make him instantly hard, and maybe a little silly. I want him to be able to go from slow, soft kisses, to white-hot passion, then back to slow, soft kisses—all without having to rip off my clothing immediately. He needed to be practiced in the art of foreplay, which should involve more than just buying me a few beers. Although, I had to admit, that approach had worked in the past. He should also be willing to experiment by trying new locations and positions—in general, have fun making love. And the brass ring is...he has to know how to give me an orgasm, or at least be willing to learn, because I'm not spending the rest of my life servicing myself.

"If I wanted to do that, what would I need a man for, right?"

"Here, here," shouted Marta, as she raised her empty glass in the air.

"Shhhhhhh. You're going to get us kicked out of the spa. It's already past midnight."

"Shhhhhhhhhhhhhhhh," she slurred back, convincing me that the combination of alcohol and hot water was finally doing her in. "So what about size? You didn't mention a thing about the size of his, ahem, member. Size *does* matter, you know."

"So are we talking length or width here, because I think width is just as important as length," I said very seriously, taking on the air of a highly-trained medical professional.

"So you're saying you'd prefer a short, wide cock to a long pencil dick?" Marta blurted out, using hand gestures to indicate short and wide, versus long and thin.

This made me laugh, but when I tried to suppress it, I started hiccupping, which caused Marta to start laughing.

"Shhhhhhh. We have to be quiet," I whispered, finishing with a hiccup. "I think I'll just add those intimate details in private."

"Boy, you're no fun," she pouted.

"I think I'm done. I've got fifty-seven basics, plus five bedroom requirements, for a grand total of sixty-two items. What I have skillfully done is made a List of my impossible dream," I said proudly, holding the damp tablet aloft. "Now what do I do with it?"

"Next, we'll have a sacred ceremony to send the List out into the world. This will summon your soul mate to appear and make himself known by shouting, 'Bring him to me!'" she shouted, as she rose from the water like a ghostly apparition with steam rising off her body.

"Shut up, you crazy bitches!" someone yelled from one of the surrounding condos.

"Go back to fucking yourself!" yelled Marta, before I could stop her.

"Shit," I hiccupped, as I hopped out of the spa and grabbed my towel. We quickly collected the two empty bottles of wine, the glasses, and the List and sprinted back to my condo before we could be identified—laughing hysterically and hiccupping all the way.

CHAPTER 4

The Ceremony

Thanksgiving had come and gone, and I still hadn't put the List out into the world. On Thanksgiving Day, I placed my usual "joke" Christmas wish list on the frig, sans the request for a man. Will spotted the omission right away, and wanted to know if I was keeping something from him. Nothing like that, I reassured him, I just was no longer looking for a man.

"Does that mean you're batting for the other team now? Wink, wink," Will teased.

Typical. I was tempted to tell him about the new and improved List, but was stopped by visions of never-ending questions and ultimate humiliation when my dream man failed to show up. So I gave him my best smirk and headed for the family room to watch some football.

With Thanksgiving finally behind me, and Christmas right around the corner, I prepared the List for its launch into the universe, where it would work its magic. The List was ready, having been re-written on clean white graph paper in perfect block printing, and sealed in double plastic bags for protection. It was rolled into a long, thin tube and taped shut to prevent unrolling. The List was ready for the world, but was I? I had to admit that Marta's mystic talk about "if I build it, he will come" and "believe in the power of your own will," and "you can get anything you want if you just know what you want," was beginning to make me a little nervous. I was beginning to become more afraid that it *would* work than it wouldn't. What if I conjured up this perfect guy—a guy who embodied everything I thought I wanted in a man—only to find out I didn't really want him after all?

It's not like shopping for clothes, when if you aren't completely satisfied with your selection, you can return it. What if, after all the energy I'd put into my List, which was up to an impossible sixty-five items, I really did find a guy who matched sixty out of sixty-five, but I still couldn't stand him? What did that say about me? I wondered. I'll tell you what it says. It says I don't know a damn thing about what I want in a guy, and dating is just one big crap-shoot like everyone says. But I didn't want to believe that. I really wanted to believe in the power of the List. So, two weeks before Christmas, I found myself in a Barnes & Noble, drinking a latte and discussing with Marta where I should "plant" the List.

"It has to be a sacred spot—sacred to you, that is," explained Marta, suddenly the great guru of List making, who was the same Marta who still hadn't completed her own List. "Ask yourself where you feel the presence of the all-powerful life force? Where can you stand, look around and get the feeling that anything is possible?"

"Home plate," I said, thinking of my grand slam homerun.

"The ballpark? That's your sacred place? It doesn't seem very spiritual to me," Marta said doubtfully.

"Think about it. Each time you come up to bat, virtually *anything* can happen. You can become the hero or the goat with one swing, and it's all within your power. Look what happened to me. I hit a grand slam homerun. And if *that* could happen at home plate, it must be a magical place."

"A baseball field as sacred ground? Only you would come up with a screwball idea of such grand proportions," she said, shaking her head.

"You said it should be *my* special place, not yours. And consider the fact that everything that has brought me to this exact place in my life has had some link to baseball. The entire reason I decided to reevaluate my life was because I was hit in the head with a softball. I was hit in the head because I run so slow. I'm slow because I injured my knee playing softball. Don't you see? Everything is connected to baseball," I explained, as if it made absolutely perfect sense.

"I think it's a stretch, but if you think a baseball park is a spiritual place, then a baseball park it is. Which field?"

"What about where we play softball every Wednesday? We could go there real late one night, dig a hole under home plate, bury the List, and cover it back up. No one would be any the wiser."

"I don't think that poor little Parks and Recreation field is significant enough for the important task of summoning your soul mate. I think you need something grander—more awe-inspiring or powerful—something like…"

"Dodger Stadium!"

Three people sitting in nearby chairs reading looked at me disapprovingly. "For Christ-sake, it's a bookstore not a library," I mumbled under my breath.

"Dodger Stadium? Wow! Now that would be a religious experience. But you'll never be able to bury something under home plate. It would be impossible."

"So maybe we could put it someplace else. We could dig a hole in the outfield, or place it inside one of the dugouts, or tape it under a seat," I said enthusiastically, picturing Dodgers sitting on their bench, unaware of what was taped right underneath them.

Marta was now becoming infected with my lunacy.

"I know. We could sneak into Dodger Stadium next week and plant your List right under the team bench. No one would ever discover it. And every time we go to a game, or watch a game on TV, we can watch the spot where the List is hidden, to see if anything magical happens!"

"Maybe the Dodgers will go all the way to the Series and that will be the magic that 'brings him to me'," I said, looking around to see if I had disturbed the readers again.

"Don't be ridiculous. There's no way the Dodgers are going to end up in the World Series next year, not with their pitching staff."

"Hey," I protested.

"But the part about your soul mate, now *that* could happen," said Marta with such confidence that I almost believed her.

It was Saturday afternoon, the last weekend before Christmas. Marta and I were sitting in my parked truck just outside Dodger Stadium, a.k.a. Chavez Ravine, which was 300 acres of excitement (at least on a game day) and sat on a small hill overlooking downtown Los Angeles. I'd never been to the park on a non-game day, so the silence was a bit eerie and the lack of activity a bit disconcerting. The all-important List was stuffed inside my jeans' back pocket. I wore a roll of duct tape around my wrist like a bracelet; had a baseball glove in the other hand; and carried a softball and black marker deep within the pocket of my Dodger sweatshirt. I started running down the mental check-list of necessary supplies with Marta.

"Baseball hats?"

"Check."

"Baseball gloves and ball?"

"Check. What do we need the gloves and ball for?" asked Marta.

"Part of the ceremony," I said matter-of-factly, as if I did this type of thing every day. "Anything else?"

"The List?"

"Right here," I said patting my back pocket.

"I can't believe we're doing this. We could be arrested, you know. I'm sure breaking into Dodger Stadium is some sort of crime."

"Look, if we don't break anything then it's not breaking in, is it? This was all your idea in the first place. You're not going to wuss out on me now, are you? Besides, I called the Stadium and it's closed for the holidays—no special events, no practice—we're clear," I said with a confidence I didn't feel. "I've seen several gates and possible entrances to the park. We're bound to find one of them open."

"And if we don't? What if everything is locked? We're not going to pick a lock are we?"

"Do *you* know how to pick a lock?"

"Well, no. But I thought maybe you did," grinned Marta.

"Sorry, but no. I'm sure we'll find something open. It's a big place. We might have to climb a fence or something, but I have a gut feeling we're going to make it."

We locked the truck and casually walked over to the Sunset Boulevard entrance to the parking lot. On a game day, entering the parking lot with thousands of other cars disguises how big it really is. But standing there, on the very edge, looking across acres of asphalt, it seemed impossibly huge. Just as I was about to take my first step out into the open, Marta grabbed my arm and pulled me back behind the wall. A small, white, pick-up truck was slowly cruising the parking lot, circling around the Stadium.

"Security," Marta said in a whisper.

"You don't have to whisper. He can't hear you from here," I laughed, even though my heart was racing and adrenaline was already pumping through my veins.

"That does it then," Marta said, as she turned to go. Now it was my turn to grab her arm.

"Not so fast. All we have to do is time how long it takes for the security truck to make one full circle around the lot, then run across to the shelter of Stadium."

Marta looked again at the expanse of parking lot that separated us from our goal. The Stadium was set into a small hill with the parking lot rising and falling around it in rolling hills of asphalt making some of our run uphill and some downhill.

"You're going to run all the way from here to there?" she asked as she gazed out at the more than three-hundred yards we would need to cover. "I hope that truck takes an hour to make it around the entire building, because otherwise, you ain't gonna make it, sweetheart."

I had to agree. So with that in mind, we decided to get back in the truck and drive around the outside perimeter of the parking lot, looking for the shortest distance between us and the Stadium. We found one spot that seemed a bit closer than the rest. But it also offered another advantage—a little island of trees and plants midway across the parking lot that would make an excellent hiding spot. We parked the truck on a side street and walked to the open entrance. Now that our line of attack was selected, we timed the truck and discovered it took approximately seven minutes to make a full circle. Marta didn't think I could make it the entire distance in seven minutes, so we planned to go only as far as the island and hide. Then after the truck was out of site again, we'd make a final run for it.

As soon as the pick-up rounded the Stadium moving away from us, Marta checked her watch and said, "Move out," just like a sergeant in some Hollywood war epic. I had only been running about a minute, when my knee started to buckle every fourth step or so. Marta kept calling out the time, which seemed like a good idea at first, but as we got closer to the five-minute mark, it started to make me even more nervous than I already was. Finally, with a full minute to spare, we reached the shelter of the island and jumped over the little curb to safety. It all seemed to be working out quite nicely—right up until the moment I tripped over the short curb and fell. The softball rolled out of my pocket, and continued in the direction of the Stadium. I got up quickly and started to go after the ball, but Marta stopped me.

"There's no time. Here comes the security guard," she said in a hushed, but commanding, tone.

Sure enough, right on schedule, the security truck approached as we helplessly watched my softball roll on a collision course. If we had been in a war movie, and my softball had been a rolling hand grenade, that truck would have been blown to pieces; it came that close.

"We are so busted," I sighed.

But lucky for us, the security guard was looking somewhere else and failed to see the lonely little ball heading his way. The near miss somehow inspired us as we let out a little yell of "Yes!" and high-fived each other from behind the bushes. As soon as the truck rounded the far side of the stadium, we were up and running again. We finally caught up with the softball about 300 feet from the stadium where it had come to rest against a tire stop. By now, my heart was racing; I was out of breath; and my knee was throbbing; but I was so excited, I hardly noticed any of it. Now that we had crossed the asphalt desert, relatively unscathed, my confidence was back, and I took charge of the mission.

"I say we stick close to the side of the building and walk all the way around until we find an opening. There are plenty of places to hide, so keep time on the truck so we have an idea when we'll see him again."

We reached the Stadium at field level and had to climb hundreds of steps as we made our way around. Because the truck circled clockwise, we decided to walk around the perimeter in a counter-clockwise direction so we could see the truck coming. We ended up going almost completely around—almost ending up where we started. If we had gone in the other direction we would have found the opening right away. We discovered an opening big enough to accommodate a Mac truck. The steel gates that were normally closed and locked on game days were, surprisingly, wide open. The entrance was cool and dark, and was obviously below the stands. There were huge concrete columns the size of redwood trees spaced evenly on both sides of the long tunnel holding the stadium aloft. We each took a deep breath, as if we were about to dive underwater, before entering the tunnel. My twin voices were both wide awake and on full alert.

I can't believe we are doing this.

It's for a good cause—true love. It will be fine.

That's what you always say. We could all be arrested, you know.

Yeah. Maybe we'd meet a cute cop or something.

We got halfway down the passage when we heard voices up ahead. This was good for an instant adrenaline rush. We ducked behind one of the columns, using our best spy maneuvers learned from watching too many James Bond flicks, and waited. Up ahead, a door opened. A warm light flooded the area around the door for about thirty seconds before we heard it bang shut. The voices had become louder, but when the door shut, they were muffled again. The sound of footsteps echoed in the tunnel. Then we heard whistling, growing fainter, so I assumed the whistler was headed away from us. This gave me the guts to poke my head out from behind the column and have a look.

"All clear," I whispered to Marta, who had a few sweat beads dripping out from under the brim of her ball cap.

We decided to hug the wall as we walked, in case the door opened again. As we got closer to the door, we could hear laughing and could see a soft puddle of light spilling out from under it. We paused and listened. All we could hear was the muffled voices of what sounded like three people talking and an occasional laugh. So we took another deep breath and sprinted past the door, where we proceeded to hide behind another pillar until our heart rates returned to normal. Up ahead, I could see the yellow glow of daylight, indicating we were almost to the end of the tunnel. We crept on until we rounded a corner to find a set of wide stairs leading up to what had to be the clubhouse level.

"Oh my God. Is that what I think it is?" asked Marta in awe. "We've actually made it inside?"

"I think so. I don't see a gate or anything. Come on!"

Cautiously, we started up the stairs, bringing us out of the tunnel, just far enough that our heads popped up like a couple of lost prairie dogs, clearing the level of the floor above us. From this vantage point, all we could see were seats. Not just any seats, either. They were the really good seats—the ones we could never afford to buy—the season-ticket-holder seats. That alone was a thrill, but it couldn't match the excitement we felt about our coming experience. We looked in both directions, checking for security, but again, found not a soul around. So we continued upward into the promised land. And there it was: the field of dreams. We saw the perfectly groomed clay-red infield, and the sweet smelling expanse of green Santa Ana Bermuda in the outfield—all surrounded by row after row of stadium seating that would rival the Roman Coliseum. The moment was magical, and we both instinctively knew not to rush it. It's difficult to explain, but it was as close as I'd ever come to having a spiritual experience. The place was completely different than when it's alive with over 50,000 fans, players, vendors, the smell of hot dogs wafting through the air, and the sound of the organ playing a jazzy version of some Billy Joel song. One can't help but get so distracted by all the activity buzzing around, that one never really appreciates the place itself—the incredible size, the vast number of seats, and the size of the field. It was simply amazing.

After an appropriate pause, we took stock of where we were—just left of home plate on the field level. Our tennis shoes made little squeaky noises as we walked on the cement floor. The high-pitched sounds bounced off the empty seats and echoed off the walls. So we made the shhhhh sign to each other and began to walk on tip toes down the aisle toward the field below. Once we came to the end of the aisle, it was an easy jump over the low wall to reach the field. The moment our feet hit the ground, Marta and I froze, wondering if some kind of alarm system would go off. When nothing happened, we turned to each other with huge grins on our faces, grasped each other's shoulders and did a little happy dance in total silence—jumping up and down, and turning in circles all at the same time. Then we went straight to the Dodger dugout, descending the stairs, touching everything with a reverence reserved for sacred objects.

"Look. This is where Lasorda always stands, with his hand on this very railing, just like this," said Marta, posing just like the famous Dodger manager.

"This is so cool," I whispered back, running my fingers along the top of the players' bench.

We both sat down on the wooden bench and took in the view, breathing deeply of the sacred air.

"So this is the view they have," Marta said with a satisfied sigh. "No wonder thousands of little boys across the country dream of sitting right here."

"Little girls, too," I said dreamily.

"Yeah, well, for little girls, it's just a dream."

"We're sitting here, aren't we? Not bad for a couple of Parks and Rec softball players."

"Why, yes. So we are!"

We sat there for another five minutes, just taking it all in, imagining how it would feel if there was a game going on—what it would sound like, what we would see. Then I started thinking about where to plant my List.

"I think I should put this someplace where we can see it when we come to a game. You know, be able to tell who is sitting on top of it and all," I said, studying the bench as I walked from one end to another.

"Let's measure in butt-widths from the left corner and place it under butt number three. Then all we have to do is count from the left three players, and your List will be under that player," suggested Marta.

"Sounds good. But let's put it under butt number four; I like that number better," I replied, getting into the whole superstition thing, which under the circumstances, seemed perfectly normal.

So I used Marta as a butt-measuring device, starting her off on the far left, marking her butt-width with my hand, and then standing up and moving her to the other side. Using this method, we determined where the fourth player from the end would sit. I got down on one knee and looked under the bench.

"This will be perfect. I can tape the List to the underside of the bench all the way against the wall. No one will ever find it there."

Then I laid down on my back, scooting my upper body under the bench like an auto mechanic going under a car. It wasn't an easy thing to do, and the thought did cross my mind that this would be a terrible time to get caught, which made me a tad bit nervous. But I managed to pull tape off the roll and secure my List under the bench. Then I pushed myself out and stood up, dusting the dirt off my hands and the backs of my legs.

"Get my back, will you?"

"So now what? asked Marta, as she brushed the dirt off my back. "What's the ceremony part?"

"I'm going to throw out the first pitch and then we're going to play a little game," I said pulling out the softball I had retrieved in the parking lot and the black marker pen.

Using the pen, I wrote on the softball, "BRING HIM TO ME" in big, bold letters and showed it to Marta.

"When I throw this ball across home plate, that will start the magic," I said, before climbing out of the dugout.

"You're going out on the field?" Marta cried in a panicked whisper. "Are you crazy?"

"When are we ever going to get this opportunity again? Even on the Stadium tour, they don't let you out on the field."

"Just wait. Before we go, there's one thing I want to do first, just in case we get caught."

Marta pulled a small plastic bag out of her jeans pocket. Then moving to the area that would be home plate if the bases were out, she scooped up a handful of the red clay dirt. My eyes lit up. What a good idea—a little souvenir of our adventure.

"Get some for me," I whispered, as I moved past her toward the pitching mound.

Sealing the bag of precious soil and returning it to her pocket, Marta picked up her glove and assumed the position of a major league catcher. Adding to the realism, she flashed me a couple signs, which I shook off before checking the invisible runner at first. Then, imitating the windup I'd seen a thousand times, I sent my first major league pitch flying to home plate. In my head I chanted, "Bring him to me," over and over.

"Steeeeeeeee-rike one," shouted Marta, before she realized her mistake and immediately covered her mouth with her glove.

We both froze, waiting for the floodlights to pop on and a hundred security guards to rush onto the field. But neither happened. So we continued on in total silence. I threw about five pitches before Marta signaled that she wanted to pitch. So we changed places, quietly high-fiving each other as we passed. After Marta had thrown a few, I stood up and motioned to her that I wanted to bat. She was confused at first, since we hadn't brought a bat, but when she saw me standing in the batter's box, swinging an imaginary bat, she got the idea. I brought the bat around and pointed it at the left field wall in classic Babe Ruth form.

Her first pitch was too high. I reached up, caught it in my glove and threw it back. Her second pitch was perfect. After it went by, I swung with perfect form and posed in the classic position of someone who had just hit the ball out of the park. Even Marta fed my fantasy by turning to watch the imaginary ball sail over her head toward the left field wall. Then I let the imaginary bat fall to the ground and began to run. I think I surprised Marta because when she turned back to home plate and found me gone, she gave me a "what are you doing?" sign with her hands. By then, though, it was too late. I was almost to first base, looking to second. As I approached second base, a single word echoed from somewhere above us in the stands.

"Hey!"

Busted! Like terrified deer caught in the beams of oncoming headlights, we stood still as statues, ready to be shot dead.

"What are you doing there?" shouted the disconnected voice.

Looking up at the 56,000 seats surrounding us was an intimidating experience. I couldn't imagine trying to play a game with thousands of people staring down. I would feel like a little fish in a big bowl surrounded by hungry cats. We looked around at the stands, but couldn't tell from where the voice was coming, which only added to our panic.

"Stay right there, you two," came the booming voice again. It was just the command we needed to make us move.

I started running first, straight from second base toward home plate. Marta saw me running and instead of waiting for me, headed straight for the short wall we had jumped over. Once over the wall, she waited for me to catch up. She was amazed to see that I hadn't followed her, but was instead, retrieving my ball, which had rolled against the backstop wall.

"Forget the ball," she shouted, no longer worried about anyone hearing us.

With only a few feet left, I ignored her and kept running. Once I snagged the ball, I made a dash to the wall and climbed over. We then started taking the stairs two at a time up through the field level. By then, I was panting hard, but the adrenaline was flowing fast. Images of being handcuffed and taken to jail kept my feet moving. "Run," screamed both voices in my head.

Soon, we were running down the stairs into the tunnel, not caring if our tennis shoes were squeaking or not. We raced right down the middle of the tunnel, past the door with the laughing people, and gave up all pretense of stealth. When we reached the opening, we had to stop to catch our breath. Bent over, with hands on our thighs and breathing hard, neither one of us said a word. We looked out at what seemed like miles of blacktop—the only thing that separated us from freedom. We looked left and right for the security truck before exiting the tunnel, then walked slowly, hugging the outside Stadium wall. We circled around to the side of the parking lot where we left my truck. Just as we moved away from the wall and were ready to make our run to safety, the white security truck came driving around the corner. "We are so dead," I thought.

"Should we run?" asked Marta, panic filling her voice.

"Run? Yeah, right. Outrun a truck? I don't think so. Just stay cool and let me do all the talking," I said, sounding way more confident than I felt.

See? I knew we were going to get caught. I knew it.

Oh, shut up. You're always such a baby. Sam will get us out of this, won't you, Sam? Sam?

"God, I hope so," I thought, as the truck pulled up alongside us. A black gentleman in his late forties, clad in an official-looking security uniform, rolled down his window.

"Can I give you ladies a ride?" he asked so politely that I almost said "no thanks" before I realized it was just his nice way of saying, "Get in the truck so I can take you to the authorities."

Without a word, we climbed into the front seat of the truck like little girls who were being sent to the principal's office—heads down, and doom written all over our faces.

"Having some fun, were you?" he asked, still sounding quite polite and cheerful, considering he was in the company of criminals.

We both clutched our baseball gloves to our breasts and just sat there in silence. Images from every cop movie I'd ever seen raced through my mind. First they would take us to some dark room in the bowels of Dodger Stadium where a single light bulb would hang over our heads. The two of us would be seated at a small table, while a huge security guard paced back and forth in front of us demanding to know what we were doing desecrating the sacred grounds. Then, off to the police station we would go, where we would be charged with breaking and entering, even though we hadn't broken a thing. And finally, we would suffer the humiliation of having my parents—or even worse, one of my brothers—called to bail us out of jail. I think Marta was having similar visions, because she was staring straight ahead, as if in a trace, with a single tear running down her cheek.

"So, where are you ladies parked today? I didn't see your car in the parking lot, so you must be out on the street somewhere, right?"

What? I thought. Where are we parked? A glimmer of hope pervaded my gloom, and I managed to point my finger in the direction of the open gate we had come through.

And then, as if by some miracle, the truck turned in that direction and started heading toward freedom. This brought Marta out of her stupor and she turned to me with a surprised look on her face that matched mine perfectly. The twins were euphoric.

See? I told you Sam would get us out of this one.

We're not free yet.

"Here you are, ladies," said the security guard a few minutes later as he pulled up to the south entrance of the parking lot. "Now, I was told to tell you ladies that what you did was very wrong and if we ever catch you in here again, without a ticket that is, we will press charges. You understand?"

We both nodded our heads and my hand was already on the door handle awaiting the sign that we could get out.

"Okay. You can go now."

I finally found my tongue and blurted out, "Thanks," as I opened the door and jumped out as if it was on fire. Marta slid across the seat and also said "thanks" as her feet hit the pavement. The guard reached across the seat and pulled the door shut, while we just stood there with arms hanging down at our sides, as if we had just been dropped off on a foreign planet. Through the open passenger window the guard said, "Get," and burst out laughing as we snapped out of our trace in unison, and took off running for the gate. We didn't stop until we reached my truck—me on the drivers' side, and Marta on the passenger's side. We looked at each other across the hood in amazement, and Marta spoke first.

"We did it!"

"We did it," I echoed.

Then we both started screaming and jumping up and down. Once in the truck, we hugged each other and burst into tears, laughing and crying all at the same time. I pulled the softball out of my jacket pocket and set it on the dashboard. Now the magic would begin.

CHAPTER 5

The Wait

T. S. Eliot may contend that April is the cruelest month, but for my money, it's February. February gets my vote as the cruelest month—not because the winter days are cold and gray, not because there are still more than two long months until opening day, not because stores are already putting out summer swimwear while most of us are still carrying around a layer of winter fat—but because of the special holiday that falls on February 14th—Valentine's Day. For those of us who are single, Valentine's Day has the potential to be the most wonderful day of the year, or the most devastating. Even if you are lucky enough to be involved with someone, the odds that he will actually remember the day, and buy something appropriate are about twenty to one—which is amazing considering the advertising onslaught that begins two weeks prior. A person would have to be totally out of touch with all forms of modern communication—including radio, TV, billboards, the Internet, even bus stop benches—to miss the fact that Valentine's Day is right around the corner. And yet, with all this help from the media and advertising agencies, there is still a disappointingly large number of men who let February 14th quietly slip by without so much as a card or chocolate Kiss. Even when your significant other does remember to buy you a token of his devotion, it often turns out to be edible panties or something lacy that could only fit an anorexic twelve-year-old.

Marta and I usually start getting depressed about the holiday around January 31st. Typically, that meant we had fourteen days to find boyfriends before Valentine's Day. On the first Valentine's Day after planting the List, we found ourselves with no love interests in the picture, and a vast wasteland of possibilities stretching out before us. So much for magic, we thought. We decided to be proactive, and invented a new holiday to take the place of the little love-fest. We planned an evening of indulgent self-pity that included mass quantities of chocolate, alcohol and enough sentimental chick flicks to keep our eyes red and noses running all night.

I was in charge of the chocolate and alcohol, and Marta was to bring over a collection of videos, most of which she owned. Around seven that night, Marta arrived on my doorstep carrying a stack of videos under her arm, wearing sweat pants, an oversized sweat shirt, and huge pink bunny slippers complete with floppy ears.

"I hope you have plenty of tissues," she said as she came in the door. "We have *Sleepless in Seattle, An Affair to Remember, Ever After,* and for the grand finale, *Romeo and Juliet*—the old one, not the one with Leo."

Yes, an evening of self-pity and incessant crying—just what the doctor ordered for two hopelessly single women. I led the way into my living room where I had set out two champagne flutes, a bowl of strawberries and a box of chocolates that were packaged in a red velvet heart-shaped box. Marta took one look at the spread and rolled her eyes.

"Perfect," she said sarcastically, "Just perfect."

She wedged herself into her favorite corner of my overstuffed dark green couch, pulled a throw pillow off the floor and placed it across her stomach, crossed her arms over it and breathed a sigh that said, "OK, I'm ready." I went into the kitchen and retrieved the bottle of chilled champagne, a box of tissues and a Valentine's Day card.

"Here," I said as I handed her the card. "I figured since you are my 'date' for the evening, I'd better get you a card or I'd never get you into the sack."

"This is why you are my best friend. You always know the exact thing to say to cheer me up."

The card was one of those clever little sarcastic numbers bemoaning the fact that we were alone, once again, but at least we had each other. Very appropriate, unfortunately. I plopped a couple strawberries into our glasses and poured champagne over them, while Marta read her card. It's truly amazing, but they really do have cards for every occasion—even for loveless people on Valentine's Day.

"I can't believe we are dateless again. I think guys do this on purpose, just to avoid having to buy flowers, chocolates and expensive jewelry," said Marta, as she set her card in a place of honor on the coffee table.

"Absolutely," I concurred. "Remember Scott, four years ago? He broke up with me three weeks before Valentine's Day and then wanted to get back together on the 17th. If that wasn't an obvious dodging of Cupid's arrow, I don't know what was."

"I can't believe *you* are alone this Valentine's Day. I thought your dream man would have materialized by now."

"It's only been two months. That's not a lot of time for the Great and Powerful Forces of Baseball to activate my List and find my sixty-five-item man. I'm prepared to wait years, if that's what it takes—or at least one complete baseball season—before trying something different."

"So is that why you haven't even been putting yourself out there? You're just sitting back and waiting?"

Marta was referring to the fact that I hadn't been out lately at our favorite stomping grounds to sample what was currently on display at the meat market.

"Pretty much. I have a copy of the List buried under my bras, and should I come across someone who even comes close to meeting the first ten requirements, which I have memorized by the way, then I will pull out the List and take this person seriously. But until then, I'm not even looking."

"Wow. You're putting a lot of faith in this list thing."

"You have to believe, Sister. Say it with me now, I believe!!!" I said in my best preacher imitation.

"I believe!" shouted Marta.

"Again, Sister. Say it like you mean it. I believe!!!"

"I believe!!!"

Then we both started laughing and toasted our foolishness with strawberries soaked in champagne, before popping in *Sleepless in Seattle* and settling in for an all-nighter.

※　　　※　　　※

The week after Valentine's Day, I had my first opportunity to put the List to the test. I never did see that Drew guy at the Lunch Box again, so I never got to explain how I hadn't *really* stood him up. But I did meet another interesting fellow named Paul, while I was trying to decide between the tuna salad or BLT. At first, I just started into my same ol', same ol'—a little casual flirting followed by a chatty conversation. We ended up sharing a lunch table that day and decided to meet for lunch again the next day. Of course, I was thrilled, as usual, and by the time I got home—after fighting an hour of traffic—I was bursting at the seams to tell Marta all about it.

After the initial chit-chat, I started in with a glowing description of my new possible man.

"So did he pass the first ten items on the List," asked Marta, after I had calmed down a little.

"I guess. I didn't really pay attention. He was just so cute and friendly, I forgot all about the List," I confessed rather sheepishly.

"Let's review," started Marta, in what sounded annoyingly like a teacher lecturing a student. "Step one—mentally check off the first ten items on your List. Is he as tall as you are?"

"Yes. I think he was even a little bit taller."

"Good. What about the age thing? That was on your List, right? Five years older or younger?"

"Not sure about that. He looked a little young, now that I think about it."

"And what have we learned about dating guys who are too young?"

When I didn't answer she just continued on.

"We've learned that they just don't connect with us, or are not in the same place on the life path. Come on, Sam. This was the whole point of the List. It was supposed to help you make good choices."

"I only had lunch with the guy," I said in my defense.

"But you already made plans to have lunch with him again tomorrow. Then you'll say yes to a date or two and the next thing you know, you've wasted two months on some guy who wasn't right for you in the first place."

"Fine," I said like a punctuation point.

"Don't get all mad at me. I'm just reminding you of what you already know," she said more gently.

I switched the phone to the other ear, stood up and started pacing around the kitchen.

"So what am I supposed to do now?" I asked, my balloon definitely busted.

"Have lunch with this guy and ask him a bunch of questions from your List. What does he do for a living? Does he like it? Find out how old he is? Try some movie references and see if he gets it. If he doesn't score high marks say, 'It was nice doing lunch with you and I'll see you around' and then get up and leave. You've got to stick with the plan or it will never work."

Marta was right, of course. I had to stick to the plan. So I did exactly that. The next day I quizzed poor Paul only to find out he was 10 years younger than I was, had no idea who Monty Python was, hated his job and was a smoker. It was really sad, since he was damn cute, had very twinkly eyes, a really nice smile and seemed to be able to carry on a decent conversation.

Over the following month, I got considerably better at using the List to screen potential dates. I'm going to assume it saved me the agony of breaking up, since no one had made it past two dates yet. So I guess the List was working—in a backward kind of way, by stopping me from dating the *wrong* people, which was half the battle right there. But there was still that other half of the equation—the part about finding Mr. Right—that wasn't really happening yet.

❦   ❦   ❦

Some people say Southern California doesn't have regular seasons like everywhere else, but I beg to differ. We have sunshine, followed by fires, then rain, then mudslides—four perfectly legitimate seasons. It was the rainy season of March, and the folks along Pacific Coast Highway were already getting out the sandbags, in case mudslides were next. With a bit of luck and a cold front, we could even get a late snowstorm in the local mountains, which would be good news for all the skiers and snowboarders. While all the rain was good for our thirsty hillsides, it didn't do much for my bum knee, which normally feels like a dull toothache, but in March, feels more like a major migraine. When you complain enough, and people suggest over and over again that you see a doctor but you never go, those once sympathetic listeners begin to turn a deaf ear. Marta can be particularly effective at getting me to do something good for me, yet distasteful—like going back to the same hospital where I already lost three months of my life, to sign up for physical therapy.

I'm a busy person, I reasoned. My job requires at least forty-five hours a week. Then there's my list of activities and commitments that always seem to take precedence over my health: softball every Wednesday; roller-blading along the bike path from Santa Monica to Venice Beach; an occasional gambling trip to Laughlin with Will; visits with my folks; babysitting for Marc and Bridget; volunteering at the Y; or my favorite past time—hanging out with Marta. It's not my fault I don't have time for a weekly physical therapy session. But Marta insisted that I put up or shut up, so I signed up for sessions. My Thursday afternoon appointment at five required me to leave work an hour early, just so I could fight rush-hour traffic along Wilshire Boulevard.

The Santa Monica branch of the UCLA Medical Center was located between 15th and 16th streets and between the Santa Monica freeway and San Vincente Blvd. Its location made it the closest hospital to the softball field where I experienced my one-and-only grand slam home run/coma, and was also the closest hospital to my condo complex off Cloverfield Blvd. What it wasn't close to was my office, which was on the other side of the 405 freeway off Wilshire, in Century City. Currently, the Tower building of the hospital was under construction due to damage that occurred during the Northridge earthquake in 1994. The hassle with traffic, parking, and working my way around construction was enough to turn my otherwise sunny disposition into stormy skies. It didn't help matters when, after rushing to get there in time, I had to wait forty-five minutes for my appointment. I was ready to complain to my therapist, Jane Carrow, as soon as she showed up but, instead, found my name being called by a tall man instead. His long, brown, straight hair was pulled into a tight ponytail at the nape of his neck and he sported a dark brown mustache that was a bit bushy for my taste. Now what was the problem? I thought. Where was Carrow?

"Samantha Stewart," he called again, this time a bit louder, scanning the room for someone to respond—even though I could have sworn he had looked right at me the first time.

"That's me," I said as I put down a copy of *People* and rose slowly to meet him. After making me wait, I thought I'd make him wait at least a full minute while I proceeded in slow motion. I'd show them. Childish? Immature? Sure, but I enjoyed watching him get impatient. See how you guys like it, I thought to myself.

"Sorry for the wait, Ms. Stewart. We have three therapists out with the flu today, so we're running a bit behind. Hope you haven't been inconvenienced too much," he said with a sweet smile.

Now I felt guilty for being insensitive. Great. I muttered something like, "Not a problem," and picked up the pace a little as I followed him to the inner office, through a couple of doorways and over to the scale to be weighed.

"Is that why Jane isn't here today? She has the flu?" I asked as I removed my shoes (a pound a piece), my bulky, hand-knit sweater (good for at least three pounds) and my purse (at least five pounds) before stepping on the scale.

"That's right," he said as he waited, poised and ready to humiliate me with those annoying little weights that slide back and forth with such ease—as if they were only little blocks of metal, not individual clumps of self-esteem.

He had started at 140 pounds, and was tapping the small block steadily to the right, waiting for the scale to balance…145, 146, 147. I wondered if he could hear me screaming in my head, 149! But 149 didn't do it. He had to switch over to the larger block, representing 150 pounds, and start again with the little tapping—151, 152…This was killing me. Finally the scale balanced at 154. Relieved, I exhaled and heard him make a little sound under his breath that sounded suspiciously like hummmmm.

"What was that?" I asked, really annoyed at having to be weighed by this man instead of the understanding and sympathetic, Jane.

"What was what?" he asked all innocent, flashing me a big white-toothed smile under his ridiculous mustache.

"Nothing. I thought you had a comment to make or something," I said still sulking at my weight. I'd lost fifteen pounds while I was in the coma (the only positive side of being flat on my back) and all fifteen of those pounds were slowly returning—like a herd of stable horses making their way back to the barn at the end of the ride. The problem is that they always come back faster than they leave.

"If you'll follow me, we can start your therapy session," he said with casual ease.

"So you're doing my session today?" I asked, still hoping he was just the guy who brings you to the therapy room.

"That's right. Bryan Williamson, at your service," he said with a shallow bow. "I'm sorry, I probably should have introduced myself at the start," he said with what seemed to be a sincere tone of apology. "As a matter of fact, I'll be taking over your sessions for awhile. Ms. Carrow has put in for some vacation time and asked me to fill in for her."

Now it was my turn to mumble under my breath, "great."

"Pardon me?" he asked. "Is there a problem? Because if there is, I'm sure I can find you someone else. Although I'm not sure who else is available for such a late session."

"No, nothing. Let's get on with it," I sighed, which triggered the little physical therapist switch in his brain and he started taking command of the session.

By the end of the hour, I really hated this guy's guts, and I don't mean that in a nice way. Bryan Williamson really pushed. He was super encouraging, almost like a cheerleader on speed—very high energy, very motivating and…totally and completely annoying. He tried to make the exercises fun, which I totally resented, and was always smiling and happy—another aggravating quality for the one doing all the work.

"Okay, Ms. Stewart. That does it for today."

I managed what I thought was a friendly grunt.

"Didn't have a good time? It will get easier, I promise. I see on your chart that you were in a coma for a couple months. If you haven't been exercising your knee pretty steadily since then, that would explain why you're having more pain than usual. We have to rebuild the muscle tissue around your knee and that can take awhile," he said, handing me a towel to wipe the drops of sweat that had accumulated on my brow.

"That's easy for you to say," I grumbled.

"She speaks! And in complete sentences. This is progress," he said with a good-natured laugh.

"Very funny. I'm sore, tired and ready to go home, so if you'll just run along and get me the sign-out sheet, I can put my initials in the little box and get out of this torture chamber you call a hospital," I managed to spit out between moments of catching my breath.

"All righty then, Ms. Stewart. We'll have you out of here in no time," he said still wearing a dumb-ass grin. Nothing is more irritating than someone who refuses to be insulted.

❦ ❦ ❦

Our softball season was finally under way again. The new leagues form in April and the first game was always played around the 20th. I was a little gun-shy during my first at bat. After all, the last time I played this game, it landed me in the hospital. I think my brothers were just as nervous as I was, because they seemed to be doing a lot of pacing in the dugout whenever I stepped into the batter's box. It probably didn't help that I was also wearing a knee brace, making me slower than ever.

"Didn't your physical therapist tell you to lay off the game for a couple of months?" asked Marta as she watched me strap on the hinged metal brace.

"He said something about taking it easy for awhile, but I'm sure he didn't expect me to stop playing the game," I said, ignoring the disapproving looks from my brothers. "Besides, he's not a doctor or anything like that."

It took me a few games to learn how to play with my knee in a brace. My first at bat, I struck out. My second at bat, I hit a pop fly, which was easily caught. But on my third at bat I actually hit a little grounder down the third base line and made it to first base unharmed, before the third baseman overthrew the ball to first. I could almost hear a collective sigh of relief coming from the dugout. Standing on first base, I turned to my brothers, flashed them my biggest smile and gave them two thumbs up. They dutifully gave me the courtesy clap I deserved.

In the final inning, while sitting in the dugout awaiting our turn at bat, Marta and I were able to catch up on what was happening since we last talked. The subject ended up on dating, men and the List—as it had a habit of doing lately. Dating had slowed down to almost a crawl, with only an occasional possibility popping up every once in a while. The List was remarkably effective at helping eliminate the people I shouldn't be dating, instead of helping me find people I should. Marta had finally completed her List, and we were discussing how and where she should plant hers.

"So where is your 'sacred place?'" I asked, now playing the part of the List guru.

"I was thinking about the ocean. Whenever I'm at the beach—especially real early on a Sunday morning when there's no one out except the surfers—this great, spiritual feeling comes over me. I'd say it's my equivalent to going to church."

"Maybe you can bury your List real deep in the sand," I suggested, thinking this was going to be cake compared to my List-planting adventure.

"That's too easy. Besides, it's the water that talks to me, not the sand," she explained. "I'm thinking more along the lines of swimming out to a buoy in Santa Monica bay and somehow placing the List there. That way it can be influenced by the pushing and pulling of the tides."

"Okay, I buy that theory. So when are you going to do it?"

"I thought *we* would plant my List this weekend, just in time for the beginning of summer," she said.

"You mean I have to go, too? You know I'm not real big on swimming way out in the ocean. It gives me the creeps," I said, remembering my near-drowning experience.

"It's really not that far. Besides, I came with you on your little adventure, which almost got us arrested, if you recall. So the least you can do is join me on mine," she said in a way that I knew I couldn't argue with. "So that settles it, we'll get up early this Sunday morning and plant my List."

"You're planting a list?" asked Will, who had moved from his position at the end of the bench to right next to me.

"It's nothing," I tried, turning my back on him to fully face Marta. I was hoping he'd get the hint and just drop it. But Marta was just dying to explain the whole thing.

"Yes, I'm putting a wish List out into the world," she started, before I could stop her.

I nudged her with my elbow and made the slicing sign across my throat but she totally ignored me. Will got up and moved to sit beside Marta, knowing he wasn't going to get any worthwhile information from me. Now it was his turn to turn his back on me.

"A wish List, eh? What's on it, and where are you planting it?" he asked, pretending to really be interested, when I knew he just wanted some ammunition to use against me.

I made signals to Marta behind Will's back to keep me out of the discussion. I was hoping Marta would understand my gestures and keep this discussion about her not me.

I didn't want Will to know that his sister was leaving her fate in the hands of some List taped under a bench in a ballpark. He would never, ever, let me live that one down.

"Well, I can't tell you where I'm going to plant it, because knowing you, you'd go, find it, and put the contents of the List on the Internet or something," Marta said, winking at me.

"Come on. I'd never do that," Will tried to convince us.

"Sorry. It's all about the spiritual integrity of the planting ceremony," Marta explained, making him even more curious.

"Can you at least explain to me what this List thing is all about? You gotta give me something here," he pleaded.

"Okay," Marta said, as I gave her a warning look to keep me out of the story.

After a brief two-minute explanation, Will had even more questions. He was definitely hooked now.

"So what types of items do you have on your List," he asked her.

Marta gave Will a short rundown of everything she could remember. She wanted a tall guy, between five and ten years older than her (she liked her men older), who was fun to be with, into sports—especially baseball—had a good job, was healthy, athletic, and available. Marta's fifty-seven-item man also had to be self-sufficient, a dog lover, a book reader and a little bit of a kook. Marta wanted someone who enjoyed the ocean, the beach and boating. He had to be able to cook, because she doesn't. He had to be a non-smoker, non-alcoholic, non-abusive, affectionate, caring, and kind. To top it all off, Mr. Perfect needed to be the marrying-type, who wanted to settle down and have at least three kids and two dogs.

"Wow, I know this exact person," was Will's instant reply.

"Really?" we both said in unison.

"You're looking at him," he said, as he jumped up and struck a ridiculous pose.

"You're such a dork," I said in disgust, and threw my baseball glove at him.

"Yeah, thanks," said Marta, who threw her glove at him, too. "You got our hopes up for nothing."

"Hey, I could be the one," pouted Will jokingly. "I really do have all those qualities—except for the cooking thing. I guess we'd eat out a lot, or mooch off our friends."

"Trust me, you're not The One," she said, getting up to take her turn at bat. "There are over fifty items on my List, and that was only a small sampling."

As she walked out of the dugout she turned to Will for final comment.

"But I'll put you on the waiting list if you want," she said. "Twenty-four out of twenty-five items isn't all that bad," she said, giving him a sultry look before picking up her bat and sauntering over to the plate.

※　　※　　※

That Sunday, Marta and I were on the beach in Santa Monica, just north of the pier. It was a typical summer day—cold, foggy and damp, with white seagulls circling around a few trashcans dotting the bike path. You could barely make out the pier with all its rides and the big merry-go-round, even though you knew it was there. Except for the early morning joggers and surfers, who looked liked shadowy shapes out in the water, we were the only ones on this stretch of sand. Marta's List was rolled up in a plastic bag and stuffed into a wine bottle. The wine bottle was filled half way with sand, and the cork was back in place with wax dribbled around the edges. She had attached a twenty-foot-long nylon cord around the neck of the bottle so it would dangle under the buoy. She had borrowed two wet suits and two sets of masks, fins and snorkels—one for her and one for me. She knew there was no way I was going in the water without one. The water temperature was a chilly sixty-five degrees. I normally wouldn't even put my big toe in the water at that temperature. She had also brought two huge beach towels for afterward, a thermos of hot coffee and a couple of croissants for the after-ceremony party. I was very impressed with the entire set-up, and the planning she had done to prepare us for the morning.

"Okay. Here's the plan. We swim out to that buoy with the bell," she explained as she pointed to a buoy that was about 100 yards out. "I'll dive underneath and attach the cord to something, then we'll ring the bell and swim back."

Sounded pretty simple. All except the swimming part.

"Maybe we should have borrowed a surfboard, or even a boogie board, to float the bottle on. Isn't it going to be hard to swim carrying that thing?" I asked pointing to the bottle half filled with sand and the coil of nylon cord.

"It's really not that bad," Marta said with confidence. "I gave the whole thing a test run in the pool at the condo yesterday. Besides, I only have to carry it one way."

With everything seemingly under control, we walked to the water's edge and put on our flippers. Then we backed into the surf, both of us complaining about the cold water. The swim out to the buoy wasn't as bad as I thought it would be. We took our time; faces down in the water, hands floating back along our sides as we kicked our flippers in a gentle rhythm. We ended up taking turns carrying the bottle because it turned out to be more difficult than Marta had thought.

We made it to the buoy fairly quickly, and with only one panic-attack moment. I freaked out for just a minute when a piece of kelp wrapped around my leg and I thought it was a fish—perhaps something worse. Once at the buoy, Marta took a couple of dives to see where she could attach the rope. She decided to dive down about five feet and tie the cord onto the anchor line of the buoy—that way the bottle was at least twenty-five feet deep. By the time she finished, I was shivering, my lips were turning blue, and I couldn't feel the end of my nose, my fingers or toes.

"Are you done yet?" I chattered when she finally came up. Her lips were blue, too.

"Yesssss," she chattered back. "Let's ring the bell and get out of here."

So we gave the bell a good shove, which barely rang it at all, but we were too cold to care. By now, the morning fog was beginning to clear. I could make out the pier to our right and a couple of surfers sitting on their boards out past the breakwater. About half way back to shore, Marta let out a horrible scream and ducked her head under the water.

Shark!

Shark!

Both of my inner voices were screaming in panic. Where was calm Ms. Goodie Two Shoes when I needed her? I twirled around in a circle looking for the telltale fin, but saw nothing. Just then Marta popped her head above water and with a horrible grimace on her face said, "Cramp!" Oh thank God, I thought, only a cramp.

I can't believe you panicked like that.
You panicked, too.
I knew there was no shark.
Yeah, right.

I swam over to Marta who had put her head back under water and was curled in a fetal position so she could rub her calf. When she put her head up again, I suggested she roll onto her back and I would drag her back in. You'd think a lifeguard would show up to save us or something, but I guess we were there before the lifeguards came on duty, so we had to save ourselves. I grabbed the collar of her wetsuit and side-kicked us back to shore. The surf pushed us in the last hundred feet, rolling us up onto the sand like a couple of beached seals. Marta was still rubbing her calf and moaning. I was trying to catch my breath, totally exhausted, but happy to be out of the water. Finally Marta spoke.

"Thanks, Sam. You saved my life."

"Not really. You would have made it back eventually," I shrugged.

"Maybe, but it's a lot more dramatic this way—adds intrigue to the whole List thing, don't you think?"

"I see what you mean. We were almost arrested when we planted my List and you almost died when we planted yours. It's that little extra effort that is going to make the List work for us."

Just then we heard the buoy bell ring. We looked out to see a huge male sea lion climbing up on the buoy.

"Look, there's your dream man, now—right on schedule," I laughed.

"Well, I did say I wanted a man who loved the ocean, didn't I?"

❦ ❦ ❦

After Marta planted her List, she stopped going to dive bars and saying 'yes' to anyone who asked her out. We both really began using the List in earnest to weed out the inappropriate dates. Sometimes it wasn't that easy, especially when the guy had two or three really great qualities that we would have just jumped at normally. Marta had one close call, with a man she met at work who left little notes on her desk every afternoon. It was a great mystery and very exciting, until she found out he was the new mailroom guy—a twenty-five-year-old surfer named Tim. Very flattering, but too young and way too good-looking. Pre-List Marta would have gone out with him anyway, just for kicks, and then dumped him after a couple of weeks. The new Marta was a lot more discriminating and was really good at sticking to her top ten requirements.

I had a close call with a beauty of my own. It was really just a slip, a return to the old ways for one night. Marta and I had gone to a Saturday night movie, being dateless yet again, and decided to have a brandy at a small pub around the corner from the theater. It was a nice little bar, not the typical pick-up joint we used to visit. There was this nice-looking man who was drinking alone, and the only two open seats just happened to be at the bar right next to him. Three brandies later, I was totally convinced this guy was The One and probably would have gone home with him if Marta hadn't dragged me out of there. Very pathetic, I know. Sex deprivation plus three brandies is a very bad combination for me. I should have known better and was glad Marta did. I did manage to sneak in one really good kiss when Marta left for the bathroom. It was warm and wet and soft and made me ache all over. The poor bastard was probably thinking, 'I'm going to get lucky tonight' since my entire body language was screaming, "Take me." Very bad, I know. Good thing Marta was there to save me from myself, because there was no way Ms. Goodie Two Shoes would have been able to stop Lauper and me from having a little fun that night.

While I was waiting for my the sixty-five-item man, I was still going to the hospital once a week to do battle with my physical therapist. Each week it was the same: I was insulting and difficult. Bryan, the happy therapist, was pleasant and kind, understanding and caring. It was enough to drive a person mad. Marta was no help at all. I'd complain and whine, and she would just laugh at me.

"You're acting like a spoiled child, Sam. It's very unbecoming and totally out of character. If you can't stand this guy so much, why not ask for a different physical therapist?"

"I did, but everyone else is booked. This is the only guy who can see me at the time I need to be seen. My only choices are ten in the morning, two in the afternoon or the five o'clock session with Bryan, the happy therapist. There's no way I can break away from work in the middle of the day, so the other times aren't an option."

"You have to admit, your knee is getting stronger. So whatever he is making you do *is* working."

"I really hate it when you point out the obvious," I said, slumping into the corner of my couch.

"You know what I think?"

"Dare I ask?"

"I think you like this guy and that's why you hate him so much."

"Oh, that makes sense. Have another glass of wine to clear your head."

"No, really. Think about it. This makes perfect sense," Marta continued, starting to get into her whacked-out theory. "This guy, Bryan, is the only guy you've seen with any regularity for the past two months."

"I wouldn't exactly call attending physical therapy sessions 'seeing' someone. I don't really have a choice, do I?" I protested—maybe a bit too vigorously.

"And you have developed a rapport, albeit an unpleasant one. You are both comfortable in your respective roles—you the whiny bitch, and he the understanding caregiver," she said, swirling her wine around in the glass, as she played the part of psychic/therapist.

"Hey. I'm not that bad," I said insulted.

"Bear with me now. What's really going on is this—you like this guy and he likes you, but because of the doctor/patient thing…"

"He's not a doctor," I interrupted.

"Whatever. The theory still works. Like I was saying before you so rudely interrupted, because of the doctor/patient thing, you two cannot express your true feelings. So you revert to the safety of your assigned roles," she concluded acting all proud of herself. "That's the real reason you aren't dating anyone else. You have a thing for your therapist!"

"Excuse me but I do not have a *thing* for anyone, especially not my therapist," I countered. "And besides, I have been dating other people. There was Larry, the divorced contractor…"

"Loser," she said making an "L" sign with her two fingers on her forehead.

"And Brad, the state inspector…"

"Geek loser."

"What about Phil? I went out with him four times."

"Oh, that's right, Phil. How many top ten items did he possess?"

"Nine," I said smugly.

"And did you check off those nine items before or after you found out he was married?" she replied, equally smug.

CHAPTER 6

The Man

Sometimes Marta can really piss me off—especially when she plants a crazy idea in my head, then merrily goes about her life totally unaware of the havoc she has created in mine. She planted the seed that I might actually like my physical therapist, and then dismissed the thought as easily as one discards junk mail. What a ridiculous thought—me liking Bryan—and yet, I couldn't get it out of my mind. The more I tried to shake off the idea like a bad pitch, the more the notion stuck to the end of my finger like warm gum. I tortured myself for hours, while working on plans for a new building we were bidding on next week. I pondered the possibility that she could be right, as I cruised along Wilshire in slow-moving traffic. These thoughts even invaded my subconscious while I slept, causing me to have a series of strange dreams. In one dream, Bryan was walking me through my exercise regimen, only we were in my bedroom wearing nothing but our birthday suits. In the dream, he had a great body and took every opportunity to press it up against me as he put me through my paces. That woke me up.

I had worked myself into such a frenzy over the idea, by the time it came around to my Thursday session, I had a bad case of the jitters. The fact that I was nervous was not a good sign, which made me even more nervous. I tried to convince myself that it was just another therapy session, nothing to get anxious about. After all, it was only Bryan, the overzealous therapist who sometimes touched me lightly on the back when encouraging me to keep going. Now, the thought of that touch made the hairs on my arms stand on end like little warning flags trying to get my attention. By the time I parked the car in the hospital lot, I had a huge sweat ring under each armpit. If I became any more nervous, I was convinced I was going to puke.

When Bryan entered the waiting area and called my name, I almost bolted for the door. All through the weigh-in and warm-up period I barely said four words. Bryan immediately picked up on my silence and began asking a bunch of questions, obviously trying to draw me into a conversation, while we went through the now familiar routine. I had been Bryan's patient for two months and this was the first time I wasn't difficult.

"What's up with you today? I bet you talked more when you were in a coma," he tried.

I just gave him a courtesy smile and grunt.

"Not feeling well? Or maybe your knee is acting up. Let's take a look," he said as he bent over to grab my calf and manipulate my knee.

My entire body flinched involuntarily, as if avoiding eminent pain.

"What was that for?" Bryan asked, surprised by my reaction. "Did I hurt you?"

"No," I said without looking at him directly.

He did his therapist thing, kneeling down in front of me, moving my knee around slowly, and asking me to speak up if anything hurt. Even if I'd been in excruciating pain, I don't think I would have been able to make a sound. During the first half-hour, a running monologue was racing through my head at about ninety words per minute, all because of Marta and her stupid theory.

First I ran through the top ten requirements of the List, my stomach twisting into one huge knot with every item I mentally checked off.

Height requirement: check—I think he must be around six foot two or three, not really sure, but definitely taller than me.

Athletic build: check. He wasn't a stud or perfect hard body, but he was definitely in shape—probably the weekend warrior type, playing all sorts of sports. Thoughts of his body as it appeared in my dream made me blush. For the first time, I noticed the muscle definition in his arms that peeked out from under his blue short-sleeve hospital shirt every time he manipulated my knee.

Age: check. I didn't know his exact age, but he seemed to be about my age, maybe a little younger. But my guess put him in his thirties for sure, which placed him well within my age-range requirement.

Twinkly eyes: possible check. His eyes are blue and have the potential to be twinkly, but this particular item requires direct eye contact of a very specific and intimate nature. I'd have to save this one for later.

In good health: check. Unless he had a hidden ailment or disease, I was assuming he was as healthy as I was.

Loves his job: check, check, check. Because I saw him at his job every Thursday, I had a pretty good idea how he felt about his work. He seemed to really enjoy torturing us all, helping us regain full use of our appendages, and making us "the best we can be."

His words, not mine. Yes, he truly seemed to like his job.

Self-sufficient financially: possible check. He has a good job, so the assumption would be that he is doing well financially. But this was a tricky one because he could be in debt or living with his mom or living above his means spending everything he makes the moment he makes it. This one would take more time to discover, but on the surface, yes, he seemed to be financially stable.

Good conversationalist: check. Sometimes annoyingly good—always trying to get me to talk about myself or about my weekend or my job. I think it's part of his job to get people talking, in hopes of distracting them from the pain he's inflicting upon them. I wonder what it would be like to have a real conversation with him? Maybe that should only be a half a check until I find out more.

Genuinely happy person, and has a zest for life: huge check! I don't think I've ever met anyone who seemed as happy and "up" all the time as this guy. Sometimes he's so damn happy I just want to slap him. You know, just give him a nice, crisp slap across the cheek and scream, "Snap out of it." in my best imitation of Cher slapping Nicholas Cage in *Moonstruck*. No one could be that consistently happy. I was suspicious. Maybe I'd only give him a partial check.

Then there was the big number ten, the Zing! How can you describe the Zing? It just happens. It's either there, or it's not, and there's not a thing you can do about it either way. I have dumped more perfectly wonderful men for no other reason than lack of Zing. It's the old, you're-a-really-nice-guy-and-you-are-going-to-make-someone-very-happy-someday-but-you're-just-not-the-one-for-me line that guys love sooooo much. It's right up there with the I-think-of-you-as-my-brother and the let's-be-friends lines that make guys cringe whenever they hear them.

Everyone sometimes mistakes that first rush of sexual excitement for Zing. It's not. Getting physically excited about someone is a fleeting thing, often gone the moment you satisfy your lust. The Zing is something totally different. Marta describes it beautifully in a story she loves to tell about being zapped by a Zing on a boat ride to Catalina Island. Her best audience for this tale is usually found at parties and is made up of other single and/or divorced women ages twenty-five to fifty.

She really is an amazing storyteller, always throwing in a few humorous asides. I've heard this particular story so often that I could almost tell it myself. It goes something like this.

"I was standing at the railing, in what should have been a very stunning pose, looking out over the ocean, watching the white caps on the sea. I was really there because I needed the fresh air to keep me from becoming ill. Another wave of nausea had just passed when I noticed someone approaching the rail to my right," she says with mock drama. "I turned a little to take a casual look, expecting to find just another passenger coming outside for a little fresh air. It was another passenger, but there was nothing ordinary about him.

At this point in the story, Marta always pauses to make sure she has everyone's full attention.

"There was this guy, a god really, who had come down from the heavens to visit me in my hour of need. He was absolutely gorgeous—thick, brown, wavy hair that was being blown about his face in the wind; huge brown eyes; pouting lips; and a jaw that looked like it had been freshly chiseled out of marble. He was wearing perfectly faded blue jeans and an old navy pea coat with brass buttons. He looked right at me and said the magic word, "Hi." It took my breath away and rendered me speechless. He came closer and asked me if he could share the rail with me. All I could do was nod my head yes. He rested his folded arms on the railing and was so close that I could smell his aftershave, Old Spice, and feel the warmth of his coat against my arm. My stomach was turning over, and a light sweat broke out across my forehead and above my upper lip. My breathing became shorter, and I felt like I was going to faint. Then this total babe asked me my name, and I answered by puking over the rail!"

This usually gets a gasping, horrified response from the listeners.

"Then this gorgeous guy, this god, this Adonis, jumped back in horror and fled the scene of my humiliation, never to be seen again," she laughs.

Then someone inevitably asks, "So what about the Zing?"

"Ahhh, the Zing," she says like she is the high priestess of Zing, about to reveal one of life's great mysteries. "The Zing came after Mr. Afraid-of-a-Little-Puke had fled the scene. I was still standing at the railing, trying to regain not only my balance but a little dignity as well, when this average-looking guy wearing a huge blue parka came outside. He was holding a plastic cup of 7-Up in one hand and a bunch of napkins in the other."

"Here," he said handing me the 7-Up. "My mother always believed 7-Up and Saltine crackers were the best remedy for sea sickness or the flu." He then took off his parka and placed it around my shoulders.

"My name's Jeff," he added as he handed me the wad of napkins to wipe the dribble off me chin. "I was looking out the window when I saw you by the railing. Judging by the reaction of the guy standing next to you, I figured you might be a little sea sick and thought you could use a little something to make you feel better."

This line always elicited a little "ahhhhh" from the female listeners, and strangely, a gagging response from any male eavesdroppers.

Marta usually continued, "He was calm, caring and not a bit freaked-out that I was looking a little on the green side. I introduced myself, offered profuse thanks and apologies and dutifully drank my 7-Up. He then led me to a spot at the bow of the boat where we could sit with the wind in our faces. He laughed easily at my story of Rico Suave's reaction to my feeding the fish, while we both munched on Saltine crackers he had in his parka pocket. By the time we reached the island, I felt much better and was in great spirits.

"He asked me if I was up for some real food, and I was suddenly famished. We spent the next twelve hours together, laughing, talking, eating, and walking around Avalon. It was so comfortable, it felt like we had known each other all our lives. That night, over dinner, in a quiet moment, he reached across the table, grabbed my hand, looked me hard in the eyes and said, 'Marta. It's been a truly fabulous day. Can we do it again tomorrow?' And that's when it happened. The Zing. It had to do with the touch of his hand, the way he squeezed it just a little, and the way his eyes burned into mine as if trying to intercept my every thought. I think my heart tripped over itself, and a smile spread across my lips before my mind could form a reply. It was—and here she always pauses, waiting as her audience holds a collective breath with her—Magical!"

Then, there is usually one woman who wasn't born yesterday or last month even, who catches on because it all sounds just a little too perfect—like a movie even—like maybe a line from, let's say, *Sleepless in Seattle*, which of course it is.

"Magical my ass! Where is this guy now?" the smart one wants to know.

With this inevitable question, Marta knows the spell has been broken. Yes, where indeed is Mr. Wonderful? "Okay," she says with a shrug. "So there was no Jeff with Saltines and 7-Up, but there was a Zing, and that's exactly how it felt—like this person was reaching inside of you to touch places you didn't even know you had. But the most important part is he feels the exact same way about you. Now, that's real Zing, and when you find that, pay attention ladies, because it's a rare find indeed."

All during the telling, I always watch the faces of the women. I get a kick out of watching their expressions change from surprise when the first guy runs away, to delight when Jeff appears like a guardian angel with his soft drink and crackers. I've heard the story so often that sometimes I even forget that there is no Jeff, and find myself wondering along with everyone else, "When will I meet someone just like him?"

So there I was, wondering about Bryan and item number ten: the Zing. Just then, he touched my knee again and I felt…nothing. Hmmmmm. Not good. But then again, a therapy session wasn't exactly the best place to measure this type of thing—the Zing thing. For the rest of the session, I was quite polite, and even a little friendly—totally not myself.

At the end of the hour, Bryan handed me the clipboard to sign out for the day. While I was signing and dating, I could feel Bryan staring at me. I handed the board back and looked directly at him for the first time since I had arrived. He was squinting his eyes at me as if he was having trouble seeing me clearly and then cocked his head to one side.

"What have you been up to today, Samantha?" he asked me very suspiciously. "You really haven't been yourself at all."

I shrugged my shoulders and immediately broke eye contact. The fact that he called me Samantha really threw me. Up until that moment, he had always called me Ms. Stewart—very professional, very politically correct.

"Nothing," I said, as I walked to the storage cupboard to retrieve my shoes and purse.

"Nothing," he repeated as he followed me to the door. "All right then, Ms. Stewart, we will see you next Thursday."

But I didn't see him the next Thursday, or the Thursday after that. On Tuesday, I came home from work to find a message on my machine. It was someone from the hospital informing me that my physical therapist, Bryan Williamson, would be unable to make my appointment time, and would I please call in the morning to reschedule. Jane, my original therapist, was back after her hiatus and was willing to take me on again, if I could come in an hour earlier. I found out that the five o'clock arrangement was not the norm, and that most of the appointments ended by five. The only good news about this new situation was that after my second appointment, Jane pronounced that my knee seemed to be back to normal, or at least as normal as it would ever be. So my next visit would be my last. She wanted to see me one more time to go over a regimen of daily exercises I was supposed to perform on my own (but would probably never do after the first week.) I needed to be tortured and cajoled into doing my exercises, and without someone to stand over me with a baseball bat, I already knew I'd quit.

Right after that weird visit with Bryan, I had a full week to wonder whether or not he was someone I could date—even though he never gave the slightest indication that he might ask me out. The twins had a field day arguing back and forth over whether or not I should even be interested.

I think he's nice. I don't see a problem with Bryan.

Nice is such a boring word.

What about the List? So far, he's doing fairly well.

I thought you thought the List was stupid? Now you are going to use it to justify going out with Bryan?

He is a nice guy.

There's that word again.

During the second week, I spent the entire day before my session obsessing over what to wear to work, and therefore the hospital, on the off chance that Bryan might wander into the treatment center. But of course, he never did. By the third week, I had convinced myself that he hated me and that's why he had dropped me from his roster of patients. The fact that he seemed to want nothing to do with me made him all the more interesting. I really couldn't blame him. At best, I had been a difficult, sarcastic, uncooperative patient, and at my worst, a psycho chick. He probably thought I was about to go postal, that he had pushed me too far. He had decided to get out while the getting was good. A typical guy—just when it got a little weird, he bailed. Of course, he would let Jane risk her life handling the nut case. What did he care if Jane was blown away? As long as it wasn't him. That uncaring bastard!

I had managed to go from curious interest in the guy, to a mild case of obsession, then to being paranoid that he hated me, to full-fledged, unreasonable anger—all in a matter of three weeks, without talking to or even seeing the guy. Yes, I was a nut case all right. Then one night after work, Marta decided to stir things up a bit. It had always been her forte.

"You know what your problem is?" she asked, not really expecting an answer. "You like this guy and he dumped you, and now you're hurt."

"He most certainly did not dump me!" I said emphatically, my voice raising with each syllable. "How could he dump me when we weren't even dating? You have to be at least going out before you can label it a dumping. We haven't even had a date!"

"Calm down, girlfriend. Nothing to get all worked up about," smiled Marta, knowing she had hit a hot button. "I just find it amusing that you're getting your panties in a twist about something you say doesn't exist."

"I was not dumped! Nothing was going on. Now take that knowing smirk off your face before I smear it off."

"Ohhhhh. Now I'm scared," she said in a tiny voice, waving her arms around like she'd seen a ghost. "Maybe nothing was happening on the outside, but on the inside, where it counts, something was going on. Trust me, major stuff was going on," she said smugly.

At this point, I took the pillow off my lap and threw it at her head, making full facial contact. Score! The look of surprise quickly turned to a wicked grin as she grabbed the pillow and flung it right back at me. This started a wild pillow fight around the living room with Marta making faces and taunting me with, "Samantha likes Bryan," in her best kindergarten-like chant. The shrieks of laughter were punctuated by the sound of pillows hitting flesh, until the battle ended with us in a heap on the couch, doubled over in pain, wiping comedy-induced tears from our eyes.

❦ ❦ ❦

The following Thursday, I arrived at the hospital for my exit visit. Jane was a little late, as usual, and came rushing in with a manila envelope filled with exercise cards. She spent about fifteen minutes explaining the exercises on the cards, and how to use common household items, such as a bath towel, to perform the simple maneuvers. It seemed quite simple, and I was getting annoyed with how long it was taking her to explain each and every exercise—especially since there were perfectly understandable directions printed on the back of each card.

At ten to five, I was itching to go, when in walked Bryan. I didn't even recognize him at first in his street clothes, so it took a few moments for the panic feeling to set in.

"Hi. Jane," he said, looking first at Jane, then turning his full attention on me. "And if it isn't my favorite patient, Ms. Stewart."

"She hasn't been giving you too much trouble has she?" he asked Jane while looking directly at me.

"She's been remarkably well behaved," answered Jane. "She's been so good in fact, that I'm releasing her today."

"Really?" smiled Bryan. "That's very good news. So after she signs out, she is officially discharged—no longer considered a patient of this hospital."

"That's right, Bryan. She's free as a bird," Jane smiled back.

Something weird was going on here. I had the strangest feeling this was all a well-rehearsed one-act play and I was the only one in the audience. I couldn't wait for the curtain to go down so I could make my escape. I felt bewildered by Bryan's sudden appearance, especially after I had so recently relegated him to the realm of rotten bastard. Bryan just smiled back at Jane, and Jane smiled at Bryan, and Bryan smiled at me before saying, "Well, I'm off. Nice seeing you again, Ms. Stewart. Catch you later, Jane," and walked out the door. How very odd, I thought.

After Bryan left, Jane wrapped up the exit procedures very quickly, wished me well, and practically pushed me toward the door. A few minutes later, I was unlocking my truck in the hospital parking lot when I heard a familiar voice say, "We meet again!" I made an involuntary jump at the sound and turned swiftly around to see Bryan leaning casually against a red Bronco.

"Sorry. Didn't mean to scare you," he said, still not moving from his position. "I just wanted to give you this flyer. It's a going-away party for Jane. She just got a great job offer in Oregon and is going to be leaving in two weeks. Since she was your therapist, I thought you might want to go."

You were my therapist, I thought. I collected myself and took one step toward him to take the flyer from his hand.

"When is it?" I asked, knowing darn well I had no intention of attending.

"It's a week from this Saturday. Plenty of time to wash your hair and cancel all your other plans," he said, sensing that I had my excuses already lined up. "Look. It's a casual deal, really. Just a lot of people from the hospital getting together at this microbrewery in Westwood. You can bring your friend Margie if you want."

"It's Marta, and I'll have to check my book. I might have to work that weekend," I fudged.

"Whatever. Just thought I'd invite you. Tell Marta that there will be plenty of eligible young men there—maybe even a few doctors," he smiled knowingly.

Well that would certainly get Marta there, but what would get me there? Then he got a little serious on me, but only for a second.

"Look. I came down here on my day off just to invite you, but if you're busy, it's no big deal," he said, before lightening it up a bit. "It's just a party, Samantha. It's not like I'm asking you on a date or something. No need to panic."

Suddenly I was no longer Ms. Stewart his patient, but just plain Samantha, again.

"I'm not panicking," I lied.

"If you say so. But you look like you're about to bolt."

Suddenly, I found my voice and shot him a sarcastic jibe, "I must say that if this *had* been a request for a date, it was one of the more poorly executed maneuvers I've seen. If I do see you at this party, remind me to give you some pointers on more creative approaches, okay?"

Bryan's face lit up with a smile. "There's the Samantha I know. Welcome back," he said before turning his back on me to climb in his truck. He looked back, and smiled again, before mouthing the words, "See you at the party," from behind his closed window. And then he backed out of his spot and drove away.

We're going to a party!

What shall we wear?

Let's wear the short black dress.

No, let's wear something new.

Shopping trip!!!

STOP IT! We, I mean me, or is it I, whatever—no one is going to any party, and that's final. That shut them up.

CHAPTER 7

The Bar

For the next week, Marta and I argued over whether or not we should go to the party. My position was that I barely even knew Jane, and the only other person, besides Marta, that I would know there would be Bryan—someone I was trying to avoid. Marta had another theory—God help me—that the whole party thing was a giant hoax, concocted by Jane and Bryan to get us together.

"Now that's even more absurd than your Sam-likes-Bryan theory," I said, finishing off the last of my beer, flagging down the bartender for another.

We were sitting at the bar of our favorite dive on Friday night, checking out the "action" as Marta calls it, while recovering from a particularly difficult week at work. I'd put in twenty hours of overtime re-working plans for a potential client and my mind was on autopilot. I don't even remember driving to the bar. It seemed like the time spent on the project had been well spent, since I heard that the Friday afternoon meeting with the client went exceptionally well and it looked liked we would get the job. There was only one hitch—the client wanted to meet with me personally sometime before the project began—something about having a ton of questions that only I could answer. It sounded a bit odd to me, but my boss insisted I meet with the guy. Considering I was happy to still have a job after my three-month "vacation," I agreed. So there we were, celebrating the end of another workweek with a few Coronas before getting sucked into our weekends. Because it was a dive bar, the "action" should have been renamed "inaction." What we liked most about the place, besides the tacky décor and absence of almost all lighting, was the fact that it was totally devoid of slick Rico Suave and preppy types. Sure, we had to fend off the occasional wino, but for the most part, people—guy people—left us alone.

"I have an idea," said Marta. "Let's throw darts to decide whether or not we go. I win, we go to the party; you win, we stay home and stare at each other all night."

"I might agree to that. Which game?" I asked, knowing I had a better chance at 500 than Cricket, since I can't hit three bull's-eyes to save my own mother.

"You choose," she said, with a devious twinkle in her eyes.

"500," I said, feeling pretty confident.

I traded in my driver's license for a set of darts that looked like they had been toys for a drunken alley cat. We grabbed fresh beers and moved to the back of the bar, where we found the single dartboard, illuminated by a bare bulb hanging from the ceiling.

Three beers and more than fifty tosses later, I was buzzed, had throwers' elbow, and was going to the damn party. With the toss of the winning dart, Marta had started dancing around like she'd won a gold medal at the flippin' darts Olympics.

"Okay, so you won," I conceded. "We'll go to the stupid party, but I'm not going to enjoy myself."

Marta shouted with glee and did a victory lap around the bar. No one there even noticed.

❦   ❦   ❦

The day of the party, Marta insisted on arriving at my place a good hour before we had to leave, to approve my outfit for the night. When I opened the door, it took her a mere nanosecond to evaluate and pass judgment on my chosen ensemble.

"No, no and way no," she proclaimed, pointing first to my silk blouse, then at my pleated slacks and finally to my flat shoes. "All wrong, completely wrong," she continued as she pushed past me and headed directly toward my bedroom before I could stop her.

She found my closet turned inside out—all the clothes that should have been on hangers were tossed on my bed. Dresser drawers were open and empty—their contents covering the floor. Marta took in the crime scene with one glance, like the professional fashion police officer she was, and turned to face the perpetrator of the crime.

"Judging by this mess, I can only assume you purposefully selected *that* outfit after careful consideration of all your options."

All I could do was hang my head like a child being asked a question that her parent already knew the answer to.

"What look were you going for here?" she continued, obviously enjoying herself at my expense. "Old-maid librarian or kindergarten teacher? It's all wrong. Wrong, wrong, wrong."

God, she could be brutal. Thank goodness I'm her friend. I can't imagine how she talks to people she doesn't like. Finally, I found my tongue and had a few barbs of my own ready and waiting for her.

"I didn't want to be too obvious or slutty, like some people I know," I said as I checked out her tight white tank top with push-up bra and skin tight blue jeans and black heels.

"You can never be too provocative," she purred coyly. "Especially in a room full of doctors."

"Fine," I said. "I'll change. But I'm not dressing like that. I'm not that desperate."

"I'm not desperate, just available—very, very available."

So the pleated slacks and silk blouse were traded in for a pair of very faded blue jeans; a purple, brushed silk sleeveless top that revealed only the barest hint of breast; and a pair of heeled sandals that made me six foot one. Marta walked around me as if examining a sculpture she had just finished carving.

"Better. Much better," she proclaimed. "Although I still think you should wear the heels," she said, holding up a pair of black pumps.

"Forget it. I want to be comfortable. And besides, I'm not the one on a mission, here. I have a List working for me, I don't have to advertise."

"Even with a List, we need to advertise a little. Otherwise, how will the sixty-five-item man ever find you?"

After making me change my outfit, she wanted to play with my make-up—highlight my eyes, accentuate my high cheekbones—all in the name of advertising. I let her have a go at it, with a warning that if she went overboard, I'd wash everything off and go to the party in the nude—no make-up at all, not even lipstick. She gasped at the horror of it all. With the wardrobe change and make-over session complete, we were right on time—exactly one hour fashionably late.

It was still early for a Saturday night, but the microbrewery was alive with bodies. Because we only knew two faces at this party, we had some trouble determining which was our little group. We finally found them in a special section that was off in one corner. I saw Jane first over by the bar, with a glass of white wine in her hand, surrounded by co-workers. There was a banner taped to the wall that read, "Good Luck, Jane!" signed by about two dozen people in multi-colored pens.

"A hoax, huh?" I asked Marta, motioning to the sign.

"An easy prop to create," she said, dismissing my remark. "You wouldn't even need to have different people sign it, just change the style of your writing a dozen times and Voila, a going-away banner."

I pushed past her in disgust and made it to the bar in one piece. With beer in hand, I squeezed around pockets of people until I got to Jane. She was friendly enough and seemed glad to see me. She gave me a hug and accepted my congratulations before returning her attention to the five guys who were vying for her affection at the moment. Just then, I saw three women vacate a small table up against the wall to the right of the "phony" good luck sign. I motioned to Marta above the crowd, and we rushed to the table before anyone else could nab it. We made ourselves comfortable and began checking out the action.

Marta and I have our own rating system that's based on how many beers it would take before you would be drunk enough to go to bed with a person. We actually stole this system from some guys we caught using it to rate us. We were both rated "no beers," which, of course, is the highest rating. But typical of guys, it was only a three-beer system, meaning that after only three beers they would sleep with any woman who was willing. We expanded their scale to include a six-pack, a twelve-pack, a case and "not enough beer on the planet."

"So what about that one?" Marta asked, gesturing with her beer at an average-looking blonde in a dark blue T-shirt and loose fitting jeans that made it difficult to fully assess his assets.

"Two beers," I said easily. "How about the guy at the end of the bar, the one with the longish mustache?"

"No beer," Marta purred. "No beer at all."

"You whore," I teased her. "Okay, how about the bartender?"

"He's not bad, but not really my type—three beers. My turn," she said looking around the bar for our next subject. "Here comes a real cutie. Maybe not your type, but cute just the same."

"Where are you looking?" I asked, swiveling around on my stool and peering into the crowd.

"He's tall, and has long, dark hair pulled into a low ponytail, although in this light, I can't tell if it's brown or black. He's wearing a white collared shirt and it looks like he's headed straight for us."

Just then, Bryan stepped out from behind a group of women and was indeed heading right for us.

"Come on, before he gets here. How many beers?" Marta pressed.

"Shut up," I said under my breath. "That's Bryan!"

Three seconds later, he was standing at our table, all smiles, with hands stuffed into his pockets.

"Hey, Samantha," he said, trying to act casual.

"Hey, yourself," was my very witty reply. I tried to act just as casual, even though my heart had been racing since I saw him heading my way.

Bryan turned and smiled at Marta.

"And this must be the infamous Marta," he said pulling his right hand out of his pocket and extending it Marta's direction.

I could tell by the look on Marta's face that she was enjoying every excruciating second of this little drama.

"And you must be the equally infamous Bryan, the physical therapist she's always complaining—I mean, talking—about," she said with her sweetest smile as she shook his hand a little longer than I felt was necessary.

I took the opportunity to gently prod her under the table with the tip of my shoe, which elicited a surprised "Hey" from Marta. Bryan just kept on smiling, looking from Marta to me, then back to Marta.

"Mind if I join you guys?" he asked, as he pulled up the third stool and made himself quite comfortable.

Before I could make a peep, Marta was on her feet and making some excuse about leaving—something about needing to powder her nose. As she stepped around Bryan to leave, she turned to me and mouthed the words "No Beers," then pursed her mouth into a kiss before finally disappearing into the crowd, leaving Bryan and me alone. There was about a year-long thirty-second period, in which neither of us said a word, followed by two sudden bursts of speech—one from me and one from him. I guess he was on edge as much as I was.

"You go first," I said.

"No, ladies first," he replied. "You had a question?"

"I was going to ask what you do when you're not torturing innocent bodies."

"After I finish with the innocent, I move on to the guilty—after work and on weekends, sort of like right now."

That was cute. So I softened a little, loosening the death grip I had on my beer.

"No, really," I laughed lightly. "What is non-work Bryan like?"

"I really do have about a dozen patients I see outside of the hospital, kind of a traveling torture clinic, if you will. These people, older people mostly, have difficulty getting to the hospital. So I go to them."

"So is that all you do, seven days a week—work?"

"Well, no. You want the whole gamut of Bryan activities and interests?"

"Sure, why not?" I said, finishing off the last two inches of my beer in one gulp.

"Remember, you asked. Let's see. I watch a lot of movies, both at home and in the theater; read about a book a month; play in a league every Tuesday night…"

"Softball or baseball?" I asked hopefully, suddenly a little more interested.

"Basketball."

"Oh," I said, trying to hide the disappointment in my voice. I guess I failed.

"Should I continue on, or should I get up and leave now?"

"Don't be silly. Go on."

"I go out with friends about twice a month, although I wish it were more often. I manage to take one really special vacation each year—one that takes me months to plan, but only lasts about ten days."

"What type of places do you like to visit?"

"I want to say I try a variety of locations, but looking back, I'd have to say my last four trips were to tropical locales."

"Such as?"

"Last year, I went to Hawaii and the year before that, Cabo and Mazatlan. Then there was Fiji—that was an expensive trip—and the year before that, I went to Jamaica, mon."

"Wow. Sounds wonderful. I have to admit I'm envious."

"Oh, don't be. I spend most of my time locally, doing outdoor-type things like riding my beach cruiser between Santa Monica and Venice Beach—to people watch—and then back again. Then there's my once-a-year trip to Vegas with a bunch of college buddies, during which I place a $300 dollar bet on who will win the Superbowl the following year."

"I go to Laughlin and sometimes Las Vegas with my brother, Will. He does most of the gambling. I prefer going to the shows. Have you ever won that bet?"

"Not yet, but I know if I *don't* bet on my team, *that* will be the year they go all the way."

He stopped talking long enough to take a long, hard drink of his beer.

"That about covers it for my exciting life—except for all the time I spend cruising bars looking for desperate women to listen to my life story," he said with a quirky little smile.

"Oh. You mean like tonight?" I asked with a slight edge to my voice.

He paused, sensing the inherent trick in the question. Being an intelligent being, and one that valued his life, he chose to take the fifth and used his beer as his excuse for silence.

"Now it's your turn," he said, after he finished the last of his beer. "I've had plenty of hands-on experience with your body, but what I'm really interested in is your mind."

He planted both elbows on the table and leaned in slightly so he could hear me above the buzz of the bar.

"Ooooookay," I said a little uneasily, not too thrilled to be under the spotlight with only one audience member. I generally do better playing to a larger crowd. "I'll start with what you probably already know, like I play in a Wednesday night softball league with Marta, my brothers and my sister-in-law. I'm a civil engineer and work for a firm down on Wilshire. Our specialty is the smaller, unique office buildings, but we're currently bidding on a new theater/entertainment center in Studio City."

I paused for a breath and raised my beer bottle to my lips, but found only suds. Bryan just sat there smiling, listening intently and absorbing every word like a giant sponge, so I had to continue. I took another breath and continued on in one giant run-on sentence.

"I like to baby-sit my niece when I can; roller-blade from Santa Monica to Venice for fun and exercise; I hang with Marta and watch chick flicks until we can't keep our eyes open; collect baseball cards but only one team—the Dodgers; I like almost anything that takes place outdoors, probably because I'm stuck inside at my drafting table working on plans all day with only one window to watch the world go by; I'm an avid fan of science fiction, including novels, movies and even comic books, but almost all of my favorite movies are comedies and sappy love stories—go figure; I like to dance, but I usually end up hurting my knee; and when I'm not busy doing all that, I spend my spare time in bars picking up on hot, sexy guys," I finished gasping for air.

"You mean like now?" he asked trying to trap me with my own trick question.

"No," I said with mock indifference, which made him laugh out loud.

"Touché," he said and got up from the table. "I noticed both of our beers are empty and if we're going to continue matching wits, we'll both need another. Do you want another Newcastle?"

"Sure, thanks."

Then he looked around the crowed bar and became very still, his eyes taking on a steely hardness. He grabbed my shoulders, looked into my eyes and while holding my gaze, said with mock seriousness, "This could be dangerous. So stay alive, no matter what occurs. I *will* find you. You stay alive." And then he turned and disappeared into the bar crowd.

Suddenly, it was as if all the air had been sucked out of the room and I was left in a vacuum. I grabbed the table with both hands because everything started to spin. I just couldn't believe what I had just heard—The Line! I stared after him, stunned, my eyes locked into the spot where he had disappeared into the throng of people. My focus was so narrow and specific that I failed to see Marta approach. Her first words startled me and made me jump.

"So what did he say? What did you say, and what did he say back? How did it go?" she shot out in rapid-fire succession, as she dropped herself down on one of the empty stools, placed her elbows on the table and cradled her chin in the palms of her hands. "What's wrong with you? You look all weirded out."

It took a full minute to regain my facility for speech but when I found it, it was like opening the door to Nordstrom's Anniversary sale.

"You are not going to believe what he said to me. You just won't believe it!"

This got Marta's full attention and caused her eyes to widen in anticipation of something devilishly wonderful. She jumped up and pulled her stool practically on top of me and resumed her position, ready to listen.

"What," she begged me.

"He said, and I quote, 'Stay alive, no matter what occurs…'" and we both finished the quote together in perfect synchronization.

"I *will* find you!"

"Oh My God!" shrieked Marta, saying each word separately, equally and distinctly and then saying it again, only running the last two words together into one "Mygod."

The twins were beside themselves.

Did you hear that? He said The Line.
I know. What does it mean?
It means he's the One.
No. It can't mean that—it just can't.
But why?
He's too nice—too boring. There must be some mistake.
I was panicking. The twins were confusing me. "What should I do?" I asked.

"What should you do? Why, stay alive, of course," Marta teased. "Besides that, what more is there to do?"

"But it's on the List! I put that exact phrase on my List, 'Will know and use the line 'Stay alive…from the *Last of the Mohicans*.' What could this mean?"

"It means he's seen the movie and likes the line, just like thousands of other people," Marta said, trying to downplay the significance, before I spontaneously combusted.

"But he said it to me. And he didn't just say it, he acted it out. He even grabbed my shoulders, just like in the movie," I said, still feeling all weird inside.

When you specifically ask for something and then get exactly what you asked for, it's a bit freaky, and a little frightening. What's that old saying, "Beware of what you ask for, you just might get it." What else did I have on that damn List, I tried to remember.

"I can't believe you found a guy who said 'the line.' You're so lucky! Now what are you going to do?" asked Marta.

"I don't know. You're supposed to have the answer to that question. I just can't believe he said it."

"Said what?" asked Bryan, returning from the bar with our two beers.

Before I could stop her with a look or a whack under the table, Marta blurted out, "Stay alive, I will find you." If I could have twitched my nose two times and disappeared I would have.

"Oh, that. It's just a line from…"

"*Last of the Mohicans*," we all said in unison.

"It's one of our favorite movies," Marta said by way of an explanation.

"I love that movie. I always end up watching my favorites over and over again. I have quite the collection. Maybe we could do a movie night some time?"

With that comment, Marta kicked *me* under the table.

"What are your favorites?" Bryan asked me, trying to draw me into the conversation.

"I have tons of favorites. It's hard to name a few," I said, still trying to stay on the outside of the conversation, still shaking inside, still not sure how to react.

"Sam and I love comedies and romances, plus a few good baseball flicks thrown in for good measure," said Marta helpfully.

I tried to kick her again but she moved her leg at the last minute and I ended up kicking the leg of her stool. Damn.

"OK, baseball movies, hmmmmm. What movie is this from? Bryan asked looking directly at me so I'd have to answer. "'I believe in long, slow, deep, soft, wet kisses that last for three days.'"

"That's too easy. *Bull Durham*," I said, acting a little bored.

"My name is Inigo Montoya, you killed my father, prepare to die," challenged Marta.

"*Princess Bride*," answered Bryan and then fired one right back. "This is an older one, but you've got to know it. 'The pellet with the poison is in the vessel with the pestle; the chalice from the palace has the brew that is true.'"

"Danny Kay in *Court Jester*," I blurted out, my competitive side getting the best of me.

"Here's a harder one," he said, egging me on and trying to draw me into the game further. "'Chicks dig me because I rarely wear underwear, and when I do, it's usually something exotic.'"

"I have no clue. Sounds like a guy movie to me," I said, looking at Marta.

"Nope. You stumped me," said Marta, looking at Bryan.

"It's from *Stripes*, with Bill Murray. Here's another one from one of my all-time favorite movies. If you don't know this one, I'll just have to leave. If you haven't seen this movie at least ten times, you must be an alien life form. 'Someone ride back to town and get a shitload of dimes.'"

"*Blazing Saddles!*" Marta and I said at the same time.

"There are so many good one liners from that movie. I could name dozens. I love when Madeline Kahn says, 'Oh, a wed wose. How womantic,'" I said with the perfect accent.

"Or, how about when the new sheriff says, 'S'cuse me while I whip this out,' and the entire town screams?" laughed Bryan.

And that's how it started—two straight hours of movie lines, everything from the *Princess Bride* to *Young Frankenstein*. Before we knew it, it was almost two o'clock and someone was yelling for last calls.

"Last call? What time is it anyway?" I asked, totally unaware of how long we'd been sitting at our little table. We looked around and finally noticed the entire hospital group was nowhere to be found, and the crowd had thinned out dramatically. Even the Good Luck sign that had been taped up behind us had somehow been removed without our notice. I wondered how we had missed that.

"I guess we should be heading out," suggested Bryan, standing up and stretching from side to side. "Where are you ladies parked? I'll walk you out."

Marta gave me a little wink. If I could have reached her I would have whacked her again.

"We're over in the lot across the street," I answered, suddenly tired now that I knew what time it was.

"Let me go take care of the tab and I'll meet you guys at the main door."

Marta and I tried to give him money, but he shook us off and headed to the bar.

"That was nice of him," observed Marta.

"Yes, very nice. Now stop making faces at me and kicking me under the table. It's embarrassing."

"You were kicking me, too," Marta reminded me. "So? Do you think he's going to ask you out? Has he asked for your home number?"

"I don't know. And no, he hasn't asked for my number," I said moodily, as we walked to the door.

Looking back on the evening everything had turned out just fine. All the nervousness had vanished as soon as we started talking about movies and guessing lines. The night had evolved into three friends having a few beers instead of the nerve-racking getting-to-know-you scenario it had started out being. Bryan caught up to us just as we arrived at the front door and held the door open for both of us. Marta took off walking with her long strides, leaving Bryan and I walking side by side. I was wondering what he was thinking—hoping that he would ask for my number, but at the same time, afraid that he would. We didn't say anything until we caught up with Marta at the streetlight.

"So? Would you want to do this again some time?" asked Bryan, a little tentatively.

I was surprised to hear the nervousness in his voice—it actually made him look cute. If he's nervous, I thought, that means he likes me. He was waiting for a response, so I reverted to what I do best in stressful situations—practice sarcasm.

"You want to drink beer and recite movie lines with Marta and me?"

I guess Marta thought that was mean, because she gave me a dirty look.

"Actually, I was thinking maybe we could leave Marta at home this time and go out just the two of us."

When he wasn't looking, I stuck out my tongue at Marta as if to say, "See. He knew I was joking." This time he sounded a little more confident, and just as I was about to answer, Marta sounded off.

"That's fine with me. I don't mind staying home."

"Shut up Marta," I said only half kidding. Turning back to Bryan, I flashed him my best smile and said, "That would be great."

"I guess all I need now is your phone number," he said hopefully.

Over Bryan's shoulder I could see Marta jumping up and down, doing a little happy dance, and clapping her hands together silently. I made a mental note to strangle her the moment we got in the truck.

CHAPTER 8

The Date

The only thing I hate more than first-date jitters is waiting for the first-date phone call. The whole "will he call or won't he call" thing is a truly exasperating experience. I'd like a representative from the male half of the population to step forward and explain to me why a man will ask for a woman's phone number and never call her. What's up with that? No one put a gun to this head or forced him to ask for the number in the first place, so why deliberately get a number and then not use it. Why, why, why? So here's what happens: The very second a guy asks for and receives my phone number, a transformation takes place. I morph from a rational human being into a total psycho-chick with a continuous soundtrack playing in my head saying, "Why hasn't he called yet? "Why hasn't he called yet? "Why hasn't he called yet?" I really want to find that little switch and turn it off, but no matter what I do, the voice begins within twenty-four hours and continues to grow in volume until he finally calls—or until I get drunk and forget I ever met the guy.

Gratefully, Bryan spared me this self-torture lunacy by calling me the very next day to ask me out for the following Saturday. It was Sunday afternoon, around four and the "Why hasn't he called me" soundtrack had not yet been activated. He sounded very "up" on the phone, and kept the conversation short and sweet, perfect for a first phone call. Just get in, make plans and get out before you can say anything stupid that might give the person something to over-analyze before the date. He locked me in for the following Saturday and told me when he'd come to pick me up. Then he suggested I bring a light jacket because we would be outside most of the time. Then he asked for directions to my house, and I guess I hesitated for a moment. I usually had a rule about giving guys both my home phone number and my address. Call me paranoid, but I think it's a wise precaution, at least until you get to know someone better. Why give a potential stalker everything he needs to harass you? You might as well throw in your cell number and e-mail address while you're at it. Then he can really invade your life. I had already given Bryan my phone number, so I was deciding whether or not to meet him at a neutral location, at least for this first date.

"Would you be more comfortable meeting somewhere?" he asked.

How perceptive, I thought. Just the fact that he asked, put me at ease. After all, I knew where he worked, and if I disappeared off the face of the planet, Marta would track me down like a bloodhound just so she could find out what had happened on the first date. Plus, it seemed kind of pointless to try and keep my home address a mystery since all he had to do was pull hospital records to find out everything from my blood type to the unit number of my condo.

"No. That won't be necessary. I was just thinking of the best directions to get you here," I lied.

So it was set. Bryan was picking me up at three, we were going somewhere outside, and I wouldn't be back until after midnight. Even when I pressed him, he wouldn't give me any more information, saying he wanted to surprise me. Two seconds after I hung up the phone with Bryan, I rang up Marta. She answered the phone with "Did he call?" Between her caller ID box and her woman's intuition, she can be annoyingly accurate at guessing why I'm calling.

"Yes, he called."

Marta squealed with delight. I could just see her doing her little happy dance, alone in her condo.

"Wait a minute. I'm moving to the couch to get into a comfortable listening position," she said. There was about thirty seconds of silence before she said, "Okay, shoot. Tell me everything."

I started with a brief description of the sound of his voice when he said hello and went on to tell her about the date plans.

"He asked me if I was Cinderella, because he was planning on keeping me out past midnight and didn't want my clothes to turn to rags. Cute, eh?"

"Yeah, that was clever, but did he say where he's taking you?" she pressed, thinking I was withholding information.

"Nope, just that I should dress warm. Oh, and he said I should bring lots of quarters. Which is a clue of some sort, don't you think?"

"Definitely. Quarters? What would you need quarters for? The first thing I think of is doing laundry or maybe playing video games but that can't be right. Forget the quarters. Let's concentrate on the need to dress warmly. Maybe you're going on a boat—maybe to Catalina," she giggled, thinking of her Zing story.

"I highly doubt that, although I'd definitely need a jacket—even in June—if we were going to Catalina. But Catalina seems a little over the top for a first date, don't you think?"

"Yeah, you're right. Maybe you're just going to be by the beach, at an outdoor restaurant, overlooking the ocean, not actually on it."

"That's possible. Or maybe we're going bike riding along the boardwalk. We both mentioned we like to do that," I suggested.

"Naw. Not romantic enough for a first date. That's date number three or four for a Sunday afternoon."

Marta is the queen of dateology. She can analyze a guy's intentions and potential just from the types of dates he plans. Dinner and a movie—the guy is playing it safe; he doesn't want to have to talk the entire date and will reveal his true colors in his selection of the restaurant and movie. Participating in an activity like golf, bowling or tennis—the guy wants to impress his date with his physical prowess, skills or physique. A bar date—taking a woman to drink beer, throw darts or play pool as a first date indicates he's not really trying to impress her because he thinks he's already done that. A homemade dinner and an expensive bottle of wine—the guy thinks his cooking is good enough to move you from the kitchen to the bedroom after a few glasses of wine.

Her list goes on and on, with detailed explanations for almost every dating scenario. I grinned somewhat wickedly on my end of the phone, knowing how much the lack of information was driving her crazy. It felt good to be enjoying myself at her expense for once. After fifteen minutes, she finally gave up.

"The moment you get home, you *have* to call me. I don't care if it's two in the morning. Just call. I probably won't be a sleep anyway, what with all the suspense and all."

This, we both knew, was a total lie. Unless Marta was out with me or her work friends, she would be in bed, dead to the world, by eleven. But I promised to call no matter what, since that was the only way I was going to get her off the phone.

The next work week crept along slower than six o'clock traffic on the 405 freeway. By Wednesday, I thought time had actually come to a halt, teetering on the hump of Hump-day, needing a little nudge before sliding down the back side toward the weekend. Thursday night after work, Marta came over to select my outfit. Only God and Marta know that I'm the only thirty-five-year-old woman who still can't dress herself. After two hours, we finally agreed upon black jeans (in case it was a dressy outdoors place) and a short sleeve, pale gray, scoop-necked, baby-soft sweater with matching long sleeve cardigan. The only thing we couldn't agree on was the shoes. Marta insisted on heels and I insisted on anything but heels. After trying on every pair of black shoes I owned, we finally agreed that I had absolutely nothing that would work, and decided that shoe shopping during lunch on Friday was my only option. How I let Marta talk me into these things, I still haven't figured out.

My lone lunchtime shoe hunt on Friday turned into an hour-and-a half shoe-fari. Finally, after torturing my feet in horrid little shoes, I found a pair of decent half boots with small heels that could go both ways—dressy or casual—and, most importantly, were comfortable.

With the great shoe dilemma now behind me, I was finally ready for my big date. I pulled out my copy of the List that was hidden in under my bras for a quick review. Of the items I could currently make a determination on, Bryan was doing very well. I counted fifteen matching items, including the still hard-to-believe "Stay Alive" quote. But that still left fifty items to go—plenty of room for disaster.

A few minutes before three, I heard a knock on my door and ran into the bathroom, to jump up on the toilet seat so I could spy on the knocker. It was Bryan, right on time. Item number sixteen could be checked off—punctual. He was standing with his hands stuffed in his pockets, whistling softly, looking around at all my dying plants in their Mexican terra cotta containers. Suddenly, he disappeared from my line of vision. I had to put my hands on the window sill, stand on my tiptoes and crane my neck to the right to see what he was doing. He had crouched down to examine a particularly shriveled up little fellow and was carefully feeling its dried out yellow leaves. Just as he was standing back up, I lost my balance on the toilet seat, my right foot slipping off the side to the floor. A loud expletive escaped my lips as I pulled down the curtains, rod and all, on my way to the floor. I quickly righted myself, peeked out the window to see if he had heard me and then checked myself in the mirror before walking to the door. When I opened the door he looked cool and nonchalant. Thank goodness he hadn't seen or heard me.

"Right on time!" I said, sounding all cheery and trying like hell not to rub the spot on my shin where I had hit the toilet paper holder on the way down. "Come on in. I'll just grab my sweater and purse and I'll be ready."

I left him standing in the living room while I grabbed my sweater and purse off the kitchen counter. I really didn't want to hang out at my condo and let him get to know me through my furnishings, my pictures on the mantel of me, my family, and the dorky poses of Marta and me from all of our crazy mini-vacations. Too much information, too soon, I thought. When I came back into the room, he was looking at my collection of Marta-and-Me photos, all in pewter frames. Guess I wasn't fast enough.

"Where was this taken?" he asked, setting the frame back down on the end table.

"That was at Papas and Beer, a great outdoor bar in Rosarito, Mexico."

"I thought I recognized the volleyball court in the background."

Purse on my shoulder, I hit the light switch and headed for the door, hoping he'd get the hint that I didn't want to linger. He did, and we were out the door, walking to his truck without delay. It's amazing how many items on the List came up just in the time it took us to go from my condo to our final destination. Item seventeen—good manners but not ridiculously so. He opened the truck door for me to get in but didn't expect me to sit there waiting, like a helpless child, while he ran around to open the door for me to get out. Item eighteen—he drives like a normal person. No Speed Racer driving antics, no riding the brake or constantly working the gas, no little leather racing gloves. There was one guy, Fred, that I dumped simply because of how he drove his car; it literally made me sick. He would accelerate, then take his foot off the gas, accelerate, and then take his foot off again. Not only did it drive me crazy, the on-and-off motion made me nauseous. Item nineteen—music selection. He asked me if I minded that he look for a traffic report. While he was station surfing, I was able to get an idea of his taste in music. It was mostly variations of old rock-and-roll and the newer stuff. There was one station, the Wave that plays mellow, New Age music. He said it was the only thing that could calm his nerves when he's stuck in traffic. Thankfully, there was no country, rap or techno to be found. We were definitely musically compatible.

I really wanted to stop thinking about the stupid List, checking off items as they arose. Every nice thing he did, every positive moment, every time he measured up, a little "check" sound pinged in my brain. I just wanted to enjoy myself and not think about his qualities and traits, but I just couldn't get control of my own thoughts. The List was emblazoned in my mind and the fact that he was doing so well intrigued me even more—like watching a game show where the closer the contestant comes to winning, the more one ends up rooting for him.

We were driving east on the Santa Monica freeway, heading toward downtown Los Angeles through light traffic. When we took the 110 north, I finally couldn't stand the suspense any longer and had to ask where we were going.

"We're almost there," was his reply.

Finally we got off the freeway at Stadium drive.

"We're going to the Dodger's game!" I said with glee.

"How'd you guess?"

"I thought you weren't much of a baseball fan? I thought the game bored you?"

"I'm not really, but I knew you were, so here we are. Besides, I still have a few tricks up my sleeve to relieve the baseball boredom. And look," he said as he reached his arm into the back seat of the truck, "I even remembered to bring a radio so we can listen to Vin Scully."

"So you have been to a game or two?"

"Sure. I just prefer playing the game to watching it. There's so much dead time compared to let's say…hockey, or basketball, or soccer."

"I guess you're right. But there's just something about being at the park—eating a Dodger Dog, drinking a beer, cracking open those salty peanuts, listening to all the people around you, being a part of the crowd as they cheer for a base hit, or better yet, a home run. It's the whole package," I said, with a passion normally reserved for speeches on religion or politics.

"I'm sure we'll have a great time, and if the Dodgers happen to beat the Braves, even better."

We pulled into the parking lot and found a spot on the opposite side of the Stadium from where Marta and I had snuck in. I had been to ten games so far this season—some with Marta and some with Will—and every time we entered the parking lot, I'd get this eerie feeling of anticipation, that something magical was about to happen. My heart seemed to beat a little faster and my entire body was on full alert from the moment we passed through the entrance until the moment we left. On opening day, Marta and I thought we saw the security guard who had escorted us off of the grounds and quickly ducked behind a crowd of teenagers until we were at the ticket gate. We spent most of that day with our eyes glued to the binoculars checking out the Dodger dugout to see who was sitting on top of the List at any given moment. When Mike Piazza sat his most perfect ass right above the List spot, I thought Marta was going to have a heart attack. I had to fight for the binoculars just to get a peek. She thought this was a really powerful sign. "Piazza Power," she called it.

Bryan had purchased really great tickets in the loge section, but being on the left field side, I couldn't see into the Dodger dugout. It probably was just as well. I needed to pay attention to what was happening in the seat next to me, not the seats in the dugout. Before we even found our seats, we bought a couple of Dodger Dogs each, two beers and a bag of peanuts. I was in baseball heaven.

"These seats aren't bad," I said, looking around appreciatively.

"I know. I was surprised I was able to get this close to the field on such short notice."

We had arrived about a half hour before game time and were able to use that time to chit chat. He kept the conversation light and funny, and had me laughing out loud a couple of times. I had to admit, I was having a good time—even a great time. By the bottom of the second inning, I was completely relaxed, which might have had something to do with the two beers, or it just may have been Bryan's disarming personality. Then, in the top of the third, Bryan announced he was getting bored with the game and my heart sank just a little.

"Now it's time for my secret weapon against baseball boredom," he said pulling out an empty beer cup from under his seat. "Here's how we play. We take turns making up quarter bets on what's going to happen next. We each drop a quarter into the cup and the winner takes all. Sometimes no one wins, and the money just rolls over to be included in the next bet."

Intrigued, I asked, "So what types of things do we bet on?"

"You'll probably pick technical stuff, using your knowledge of the game to gain an unfair advantage—something like a certain player will get a base hit or the pitcher will strike him out. I, on the other hand, like to go for more non-baseball related bets, like how many times will the pitcher adjust his ball cap in the next inning; weird stuff like that."

"You go first, so I can get the hang of it," I said.

"Here's the first bet. Starting now, how many times will the third baseman do that dirt-moving thing with his foot in this inning? Whoever gets closest to the right number wins. Ante up," he said and held the plastic cup out for me to deposit my quarter.

I bet the third baseman would move the dirt around three times and Bryan bet five. Then we spent the next inning with our eyes glued to the third baseman, good-naturedly arguing over whether something was a true swipe of the dirt or whether he had just moved his foot a little. By the end of the inning, the count was at four, so the quarters stayed in the cup for the next bet. Now it was my turn. My bet was that the next out would be caused by a fly ball. With the crack of the bat, I lost four quarters as centerfielder Marquis Grissom grounded out on the first pitch. Bryan was thrilled and made a huge deal of collecting the money from the cup, even standing up to do a little victory dance.

The quarter bets continued: how many total balls would be thrown in an inning; what was the evening's attendance; how many times would Vin Scully mention some type of Farmer John meat product on the radio; and my personal favorite, how many times would the pitcher adjust himself in one inning? The amazing answer to that one was ten times! Bryan didn't like that bet because it forced him to watch the pitcher's crotch the entire inning. Marta would have loved that one. At the bottom of the ninth inning, we were betting on what type of out would end the game, a fly ball, a ground ball or a strike out. There were six quarters in the cup, the biggest single winnings of the night. I picked a fly ball to end the game and Bryan picked a grounder.

"The count is three and one; here's the wind-up and the pitch," narrated Bryan. "He swings, and bam! He whacks a good one into left field. Klesko is charging the ball. Will he make it in time? Looks like he's going to be short. But, no. He dives. And yes, he has the ball. The last out of the game is a fly ball."

"I win, I win," I squealed as I jumped up and down.

The people around me were all giving me dirty looks, since the Dodgers ended up losing four to five with that out. But I didn't care. I was a whole $1.50 richer! So what if it wasn't a lot of money? The thrill of winning made it fun. Bryan started laughing at my antics and graciously poured the six quarters into my outstretched hand.

"Congratulations to the big winner of the night," he said and leaned over to give me a light kiss on the cheek.

Before I could react, he grabbed my hand and was leading me up the aisle.

"Come on. We've got to get moving or we're going to miss part two of the evening," he explained as he led me through the crowds.

"Part two?"

"Yes. Part one was the baseball game, something I thought you would enjoy. Part two is something I know I will enjoy."

Immediately I thought the worst. If this guy thinks I'm just going to fall into the sack with him after a few beers and a Dodger Dog or two, he's in for a big shock. I could feel my body tense as I prepared myself for the same old ugly scene I've played out over and over again. Bryan must have felt the change in my body language because he began to shake my hand and wiggle my whole arm like it was a giant noodle.

"Relax. It's not what you think. We're not going back to my place or even your place for that matter," he said, smiling easily.

"That's not what I was thinking," I lied.

"Good. I'm taking you to one of my favorite places in L.A. It's only twenty minutes from here—that's twenty minutes after we get out of the parking lot," he said, looking at the huge traffic jam of cars heading for the exits.

With some creative maneuvering, we got out of the parking lot in record time, taking the Sunset Boulevard exit heading west. I had absolutely no clue as to where we were heading, until we turned onto Hillhurst and crossed Los Feliz going up into the hills of Griffith Park.

"I'm going to make a guess. We're headed for the Observatory, right?"

"Gee, you are just too smart for me."

"But it's almost nine. Will it still be open?"

"Fear not, gentle lady. They are holding the place open just for us. Tonight, Samantha, I will present to you on a black porcelain platter, the stars of the universe, at least all the ones we can see from here."

"That's it, stars?" I said teasing him. "Most guys give me expensive jewelry on the first date."

"I give you stars, and these," he said pulling something out of his jacket pocket.

"What's this?" I asked, taking a white Dodger gift bag from his hand.

"Open it."

Slowly, I opened the little white bag and found three packets of Dodger baseball cards.

"Hey, how did you know?" I asked, turning the cards over in my hand before ripping the cellophane open with my teeth and flipping through the cards.

"You told me that night at the bar that you collect baseball cards, Dodger cards to be specific. Are there any good ones in there?"

"Here's an old Don Drysdale and a Dusty Baker card from 1977. I don't think I have either of these. This is great. When did you buy them?"

"When I went up to get our second round of beers."

"Very impressive," I said, flipping through the rest of the cards.

Just then, we pulled into the practically deserted parking lot of the Griffith Park Observatory. The Observatory is located on the southern slope of Mount Hollywood, above Hollywood and Los Angeles. On a clear night, the location affords fabulous views of the city lights below. Those same city lights make viewing the night sky without the aid of a powerful twelve-inch telescope a waste of time. We walked to the edge of the parking lot for our first view of the city lights and somewhere along the way, Bryan draped his arm over my shoulder, so naturally, it didn't even register at first. We stood in silence overlooking the city for a full minute before both of us said, "Beautiful" at the very same time. It was surprisingly comfortable, standing there on the edge of L.A., not saying a word, just looking at the city lights and thinking our own private thoughts. I was glad he didn't feel the need to talk or ruin the moment by trying to kiss me. It just felt good exactly the way it was. After about five minutes Bryan finally broke the silence.

"Come on," he said, leading me away from the view and walking me along the sidewalk toward the Observatory. "I promised you the stars and I mean to deliver—the observation deck closes in twenty minutes."

The Observatory has three domes protruding above the roof line. One houses a solar telescope, one is the ceiling for the planetarium show and the third houses the telescope where we were heading. Two sets of gently spiraling staircases, on either side of the white-washed building, hug the outside edge as it curls up to the roof. The Observatory building has architectural features reminiscent of the beautiful buildings of Greece. A running geometric pattern, along one of the back walls, was an exact replica of a design I'd seen recently on a picture of Greek pottery. I was as fascinated by the building, as I was by the spectacular views provided by the unique locale above both Los Angeles and Hollywood.

That night, the resident astronomer had the telescope trained on the rings of Saturn. Because of all the glare from the city, the moon and planets were the best night sky objects to see from this location. There was only a short line—about six people—waiting to look through the telescope. When it was my turn, I climbed the dozen wooden steps to the viewing platform and pressed my eye into the eyepiece. It was amazing. Until that moment, I'd never really seen the night sky—never seen it like that. It was so beautiful and humbling, all at the same time. It literally made me gasp. From the moment I climbed down, until we were back in Bryan's truck, I couldn't stop talking about the incredible beauty of the planet, its rings, and the possibility of life on other planets. When I stopped for two seconds to catch my breath, Bryan found the opportunity to jump right in.

"So I gather you liked my little surprise?" asked Bryan, as he opened the truck door for me.

"Oh, my God, I loved it. I've never seen the night sky like that before," I practically gushed.

Bryan walked around and got into the driver's side door but didn't start the engine right away.

"So, what was better, part one, the baseball game, or part two, the Observatory? I'd kind of like to know for future adventures," he said.

"Hmmm. That's a tough one. The game was really fun and it did involve baseball, which I love, and Dodger Dogs, which are hard to beat, and there was of course, the beer. But the Observatory was a totally new experience for me, so it had a certain fresh excitement that the ball game was missing. And how can a baseball game compete with a million billion stars? I'd have to say it's a tie. I really enjoyed both parts, one and two."

"Well, maybe this will help break the tie," he said, as he leaned across the seat and kissed me ever so gently on the lips.

A small zing went shooting through my body and made me feel tingly all over. It wasn't the capital "Z" zing, but a lowercase zing—one that can be attributed to pure physical pleasure. Not that that was bad. Pure physical pleasure is nothing to take lightly and is extremely enjoyable, but it is just a physical reaction—not the mental/emotional/spiritual Zing of storybook fame. The nicest thing about the entire moment was that he left it at that, one perfect kiss, which left *me* wanting more. No groping, or slobbering or jamming of tongue down throat on the first attempt. The perfect kiss for the moment and for a first date. When he pulled away, we were both smiling.

"Shall we go?" he asked, his hand already reaching for the keys in the ignition.

"I think so," I said, not wanting to ruin a perfect evening.

And with that, he started the truck, adjusted the radio to a classic rock station and wound back down the mountain. At eleven thirty on a Saturday night, there was only light traffic, and we made it back to my place in record time.

Let's ask him in.
Absolutely not.
I think we should kiss him again—a real kiss.
That would be okay—but that's all.
Don't we need to find out if he's good at other "things" as well?
Yes, but not tonight. Just one more kiss, and that's all.
You are no fun.
As Bryan was walking me back to my condo, he took a glance at his watch.

"Darn, it's 11:55. I got you home before midnight, Cinderella."

"Why darn?" I asked.

"Because now I don't get to watch your clothes turn into rags."

"Sorry to disappoint you, Prince Charming, but you'll just have to wait until next time."

"So that means there will be a next time?" he asked hopefully.

"Well, there is that part when you're supposed to come around with a glass slipper and all."

"Oh, that's right—the glass slipper. So I guess it would be all right to call you and ask your shoe size then?" he inquired, right as we got to my front porch.

"Size eight."

And with that, he made his move for the big goodnight kiss. Putting his arm around my waist, he pulled me close in one smooth move. He paused just a moment to look into my eyes before tilting his head slightly and pressing his parted lips into mine. I felt my body melt and my lips go soft, as he gently moved his mouth on mine. He gently explored with his tongue, while massaging the back of my neck with his free hand. Then, just as the temperature of our bodies was starting to rise, he slowly pulled back, smiled and said, "Thank you for taking a chance and going out with me."

"Thank you. It was a wonderful first date," I said quietly, not wanting to break the enchantment of the moment.

He gave me one more kiss before letting me go. He waited while I found my key and unlocked my door. I stepped through the opening and turned for one more good-bye.

"Thanks again," I said. "It really was a terrific date—both parts, one and two."

"It was my pleasure." And then glancing at the bathroom window, he said with a devilish smile, "If you need any help fixing that curtain rod, just give me a call." And then he stuffed his hands into his pockets, did an about-face and was gone.

CHAPTER 9

The Test

Seven dates and two months later, Bryan and I were still going out. He seemed to be taking it as slow as I was, and had kept all of our dates in what Marta would call the adventure category. Date number four was a bike ride to Venice Beach, just as Marta had predicted, and date number five was a day at the L.A. Zoo, where we spent an entire hour laughing at the antics of the gibbons. I had just gotten home from date number seven, which was an outdoor Mozart concert at the Hollywood Bowl and probably the most romantic of all of our dates so far. I couldn't wait to call Marta with my report.

As soon as Bryan left, I was on the phone, waiting for Marta to pick up. I glanced at the clock on my nightstand and realized she was probably sound asleep. After the seventh ring, a very sleepy-sounding Marta picked up the phone.

"Hello?"

"Marta, it's Sam. I'm checking in after my date," I said, hoping to awaken her a little.

"What time is it?"

"Only one-thirty, still pretty early."

"Did you do the wild thing?" she asked hopefully.

"Nope."

"Oh," she said, then hung the phone up.

I hadn't expected that reaction. I sat on the edge of the bed looking at the phone for a full ten seconds, deciding whether or not to call her back. Finally I placed the receiver back in its cradle. No, I hadn't slept with Bryan yet. So what? We were taking it real slow, which I liked. I don't think he wanted to move any faster, either, since he was the one who kept all the dates more like adventures than romantic liaisons. But Marta thought that after four dates if you weren't sleeping together or doing the "wild thing" as she called it, then something was wrong. I, on the other hand, wanted to make sure there was a true relationship and that both people were playing by the same set of rules before bringing the bedroom into the picture. I'd been burned too many times by assuming that I was in an exclusive relationship—only to find out the guy was dating, and sleeping with, several other women at the same time. Yuck! Call me old-fashioned, but I think sleeping with multiple partners is both disgusting, and nowadays, dangerous—even deadly. I went to bed thinking about all this stuff and consequently, didn't sleep well at all.

The next morning, I called Marta early, looking for a little payback for her behavior last night, but a bright, chipper Marta answered the phone and took the punch right out of me.

"So how's my favorite person on the planet today," Marta chirped.

"Not bad. You sound better than last night."

"Last night? Did I talk to you last night?" asked Marta.

"You don't remember our charming conversation?"

"Can't say I do. I must have been asleep. What did I say?"

"Oh, the same old, same old, 'Did you do the wild thing?'" I mimicked.

"Well, did you?" she asked again.

"No, and if you hang up on me this time I'm going to come over there and slap you," I said testily.

"Sounds like someone got up on the wrong side of the bed this morning," she said in a baby voice. "Why so touchy?"

"Just tired of that being the only thing you are interested in these days. It's not just me; neither one of us wants to rush it," I said defensively.

"Stay right there, I'm coming over."

And before I could protest, she had hung up on me again. Ten minutes later she was at my door wearing her Ugg boots, flannel boxers and a sweatshirt, with a pot of coffee in one hand and a bag of bagels in the other.

"I knew you wouldn't have any decent coffee, so I brought my own," she said, as she made her way into the kitchen.

"Make yourself at home," I said sarcastically, following her to the table.

She went directly to the cupboard where I kept the coffee cups and pulled out two huge mugs. She poured us each a full cup and placed them on the kitchen table. Then she opened a drawer, pulled out a serrated knife and cut two bagels up into bite-size pieces. Opening the refrigerator, she rummaged around until she found the cream cheese and placed that on the table with a knife. Bringing the bagel pieces with her, she finally sat down at the table, pulled a chair into position for her feet and sighed a contented sigh.

"Comfy?" I asked.

"Perfect. Now what's this about you and Bryan not sleeping together yet? It's been, what, two months? That's got to be a record for you," she said, before dabbing a bit of cream cheese on one of the bagel pieces.

"I really don't know why we haven't gone there yet. It just hasn't come up," I said, turning the cream cheese knife vertically to emphasize the word 'up.' "We've been having so much fun dating. Maybe we're both afraid to take it to the next level. What if it ruins everything?"

"It's not going to ruin anything. What good is this great friendship if it doesn't go anywhere? That's what the List was all about—helping you know what you want, so you can recognize it when it's sitting in your living room. How's he doing on the List, anyway?"

"Amazing! He's ninety-eight percent on the items I've been able to check off, and well over fifty percent on the entire List, which includes the ten items that only pertain to the bedroom. As we know, I can't evaluate those yet."

"So what are you waiting for?" asked Marta, as she wiped a little cream cheese off her upper lip.

"It's the Zing thing," I said sadly. "We just haven't had that moment yet, and it's driving me crazy."

"Not the no-Zing-thing. Damn. And he's such a perfect guy for you."

"You think so? I've had lower case 'z' zings—little physical bursts of "ohhh-hhhhhh," but then nothing happens after that. Remember the day he surprised me at work with the glass slipper after our first date?"

"How could I forget that? It was so romantic. You were dancing on air that day."

"I thought I had the big Zing then, but now I think it was just the excitement of the gift, the romance of it all, and the way he was so thoughtful and nice. I just don't have the desire to rip his clothes off and rape him like I used to get with some guys."

"Yes, but if you recall, all the guys you felt that way about were losers! Maybe he's just shy, or trying not to push you. Maybe you need to invite him over for a romantic dinner," she suggested.

"No," I said forcefully. "I don't want to orchestrate an evening that has the sole purpose of getting Bryan into bed. That seems too manipulative. And whenever I've forced a situation in the past, it's been disastrous."

"Guys never think that. When a guy walks into a room lit only by candles, with glasses of wine on the table and their woman in a slinky dress, do you really think they are going, 'That manipulative little bitch'? I'd bet my entire collection of antique silver spoons they're doing a little happy dance of their own, thinking 'Wake up Boys! We're getting lucky tonight!'"

"Yeah, you're right. But I still don't want to force anything. If it's meant to be, it will happen. Otherwise, we're having a wonderful time, and there's nothing wrong with that."

❦   ❦   ❦

Three weeks later, I was still dating Bryan and we still weren't having sex. Even the twins were complaining.

What's up with this Bryan guy? He hasn't even made The Move.

Maybe he's being polite?

Polite? Since when are guys polite about sex? Anxious, over-eager, pushy, and demanding—yes, polite—no.

I don't know. I think he's nice, though.

There's that word again, "nice."

There's nothing wrong with nice.

Maybe he's a sexual deviant and is afraid once Sam sees that side of him she'll bolt.

That's hard to imagine.

Exactly. You know, he can't be The One, if he can't perform in bed. Maybe he knows something we don't.

That's pretty harsh. What if he possesses fifty-five out of sixty-five items on the List—everything but the ten bedroom qualities? Are we going to reject him based on lack of sex.

You bet we are. If we didn't, we might as well marry Marta!

Bryan had just asked me out for Friday night, when the phone rang again. I was at work and it was about two in the afternoon on a Tuesday. The voice was from someone I didn't recognize. It had a deep timbre and a slight accent, Spanish, I thought, like a Palm Spring breeze. He introduced himself as Marcos Arlando, the owner of the soon-to-be-built theatre complex in Studio City.

This was the guy who had all the questions. He had been trying to get together with me for months now but our schedules never seemed to match up. He had been traveling out of the country for the past two weeks and was due to leave for Spain again next Sunday, he explained. Friday night was the only night he could make it and he practically begged me to meet him for a business dinner. I reluctantly said yes, and then had to call Bryan back immediately to try to move our date to Saturday night. As it turned out, he was going out with his buddies from the hospital Saturday night, so we made plans to meet for Sunday brunch. Mr. Arlando suggested we meet at a tapas bar in Westwood, the college town surrounding UCLA. It was a good place to meet, considering it was on my way home and I wouldn't have to fight too much traffic to get there.

That day, I wore my standard meet-a-client attire, consisting of my black jeans and a crisp, white shirt that I wore untucked, reaching down to midthigh. I had never met Mr. Arlando and was expecting an older gentleman—both from the sound of his voice and the fact that he could afford to build the type of entertainment center I had designed. I was wrong, very wrong. Marcos Arlando wasn't old at all.

When I entered the restaurant, he was sitting at the bar, facing the door. As soon as I walked in, he was on his feet moving in my direction. He was tall, at least six foot three, with jet-black hair and dark brown eyes. He looked like a Spanish matador without the red cape. He stepped right in front of me and in that same deep voice said, "And you must be the lovely Samantha Stewart," as he pulled a red rose out from behind his back and presented it to me. My brain was sputtering like an old car trying to turn over on a cold morning. This was supposed to be a business meeting, yet it had all the trappings of a date.

After what seemed like an embarrassingly long pause, I found my voice and professional bearings. I took the rose deliberately with my left hand so I could extend my right for the usual business handshake.

"And you must be Mr. Arlando," I said reaching out to shake his hand.

"You must call me Marcos, I insist," he said, rolling the "r" ever so slightly.

Then he took my hand turned it, and pressed his lips onto the back of my hand, lingering there long enough to make me nervous. An involuntary shudder ran through my body, which I hoped he hadn't noticed.

"If you will follow me," he continued in that dreamy voice, "I have a table all ready for us. I hope you brought the plans. I'm very excited to go over them with you."

"Got them right here," I said briskly, all professional and in control again as I patted the large leather satchel hanging from my shoulder.

"Here, let me carry that for you." And before I could protest, he had pulled the satchel off my shoulder and was walking toward the rear of the restaurant to our table.

The table was actually a small, two-person booth tucked in the furthest corner of the restaurant. The lighting had an orange-red tint that was a result of the stain glass sconces on the wall. The rolled leather booth was upholstered in a deep brick red and was cold to the touch but the dark wood of the table and walls made the entire area seem warm and inviting. Great date location, horrid place to review plans, I thought. We sat across from each other and as soon as I had spread my napkin on my lap, I pulled my case onto the table and started to open it, but Mr. Arlando gently grabbed my hand and stopped me.

"I need a few moments before launching into business. First a drink, a few tapas, and then we'll look at the plans."

I shrugged my shoulders and removed my hand. This was a weird situation. He was a client, so business rules dictated I let him control the direction of the meeting. But he wasn't acting like any client I had ever met, and I found myself constantly second-guessing what he meant by everything he said.

"I did not expect that the engineer on my project would be a woman—a woman of such outstanding beauty and grace," he said leaning forward slightly in his chair.

I had to fight the urge to look around to see who he was talking about. Alarms began going off inside my head; the twins were instantly on full alert.

Mayday, mayday, business meeting in a tailspin. Pull up, pull up.

Relax. It's just a little meeting. So what if the client is drop-dead gorgeous. We can handle him.

Yeah, right.

I thought I'd try a little of my infamous sarcasm to bring Mr. Arlando back to the real world.

"I'm pretty sure you knew I was a woman. Although maybe it's perfectly normal for you to bring a red rose to all your business meetings," I quipped. "And of course we did speak on the phone."

"Ohhhh. And witty, too. What a find! You are right, of course. I must confess, I have been to your office several times. Each time, you were hunched over your drafting table intent on your work. I was very impressed by your level of concentration—never once did you lift that perfect chin to look around the room. I was intrigued. I wanted to meet the woman behind the plans."

Just then the wine steward came by with the wine list. As client/vendor relationship dictated, I tried to grab the wine list, but Mr. Arlando would have none of that.

"Mr. Arlando, I insist. You are a client of my company and I will be buying dinner this evening. After all, this is a business meeting," I said with as much authority as I could muster in the darkened restaurant.

"That's very kind of you, but of course, I will be paying for everything this evening. It was I who invited you out, and you are my guest here. My brother owns this restaurant, so if it makes you feel any better, it won't be costing me a cent either," he said with such a charming smile that even the wine steward appeared to melt.

He selected a bottle of wine and then turned his full radiance on me. It was almost blinding, even in the dark recesses of our booth.

"If we are going to get along this evening, you'll need to do one very important thing for me. You must call me by my first name, Marcos. To me, Mr. Arlando is my father," he said, charm just dripping off of his full, very kissable lips.

"I think I can do that, but you'll still need to call me Ms. Stewart."

"Really?"

"No. I was just kidding. You can call me Samantha if you want."

When the wine arrived, Marcos went through the entire swirling, inhaling, sipping thing before he approved. After two glasses, I was well on my way to forgetting why I was there—the wine was *that* good. He did the whole, "So, tell me about yourself," and I obliged—although in brief—because to tell the truth, I was much more interested in finding out about him. The entire time I was talking, he didn't take his eyes off of me. At first, his intensity was disturbing. I felt like a bug under a microscope, what with him absorbing my every expression and hand gesture. But after the wine kicked in, it didn't seem to bother me as much, and I actually grew to enjoy it. Once he started talking, he spoke in slow, smooth rhythms about his childhood in Madrid and how he and his brother had moved to the States when he was twelve with their uncle. Listening to him talk was like floating down a slow moving river, not really caring where you were going or when you would get there but simply enjoying the ride.

I think it was some time after the second bottle of wine that I finally realized he was holding my hands in his at the middle of the table. The twins must have been drunk, too, because they were curiously silent. I recall wondering how long this had been going on. I looked around the table and saw a dozen little plates with bits of food on them, but I couldn't remember eating or what I ate. At some point we actually looked at the plans. I remember him questioning several insignificant details while using the moment as an excuse to lean over the plans and into me. As I was leaning over the plans, pointing out certain design features that were causing some problems, my hair fell across my face. Marcos gently took his hand and pulled the hair out of my eyes and tucked it lovingly behind my ear. Electrical currents made a direct connection between the place on my ear where his fingers brushed my skin and the place between my legs that was already buzzing from all the wine and his sexy voice.

We knew it was time to go because the lights were coming on in other areas of the restaurant. I looked at my watch and was amazed to find that it was well past midnight. A thought struck me, and I looked down at my clothing to see if they had turned into rags. Nope. I giggled to myself at the thought.

"Something funny you'd like to share," asked Marcos, who was a little tipsy as well.

"I was just checking to see if my clothes had turned into rags."

"Why? Has that happened to you before," he asked, looking very puzzled, not getting the reference to Cinderella at all.

Bryan would have gotten it right away, I thought, as I tried to stand up with a grace I didn't feel.

"Looks like someone's had a little too much wine. I think I will have to drive you home," he said hopefully.

"I don't think so, Mr. Arlandoooo," I said in what I hoped would be a sober-sounding voice.

"No, really. You are in no condition to drive home. At least let me call you a cab."

And with that, he signaled the last remaining waiter, who was waiting for us to leave, and asked him to call "us" a cab. The "us" part didn't register at first. Not until he was climbing into the cab behind me did it really sink in that we were sharing a cab.

"You're coming with me?" I asked, somewhat shocked.

"But of course. I would never leave a beautiful woman such as yourself in the hands of a mere cab driver. I will make sure you arrive home safely, and then I will go home myself."

It was too late to argue, since we were already pulling away from the curb. I vaguely recall wondering how I was going to get my car back before allowing myself to relax. When I leaned forward to give my address to the cab driver, Marcos stretched his arm along the back of the seat. Smooth move—a little too smooth—I thought. With his arm now around my shoulders, he began gently massaging my shoulder. This had the twins awake and on their feet at last.

This is not good, definitely not good.

It's fine. It feels good. What's the harm of a little rubbing?

What? Are you suddenly stupid? A little rubbing turns into a lot of rubbing.

There, he stopped rubbing, so stop your worrying.

Yeah, but now he's squeezing and applying pressure. He wants you to turn toward him. Don't do it, Sam. This is a business meeting.

Who are you kidding? The moment he whipped out that red rose you knew it wasn't about business. I'm going to turn.

It's a mistake!

When I turned to face him he leaned into me and, with his free hand, cupped my chin. Then for a whole ten seconds he just looked into my eyes and then at my lips.

Oh, my God. He's going to kiss you. Turn away, turn away. Before it's too late.

Shut-up. I want him to kiss me.

What about Bryan?

What about him?

And at that moment, I really did want him to kiss me. The second I decided, he saw it in my eyes and pulled me in close. Then he grabbed my lower lip with his teeth and gently nibbled on it before exploring my mouth with his. He pressed harder, moving his hand from my chin to my back and pulled me on top of him as he leaned back against the cab door.

I can't believe this. What are you doing?

We're having a little fun. Go back to sleep, princess. I'll take over from here.

Like hell you will.

Yeah. Just a little fun, I thought as I let the physical sensations block out all arguments and brain static. He kissed me deeper and deeper, while his hands pressed against my back, grabbed my ass, and pressed me into him so that I could feel his hardness. My body was responding in a hundred different ways and I was in danger of loosing some clothing very soon if I didn't slow things down.

Suddenly it dawned on me that we had been stopped for quite some time. I pulled myself back to an upright position and saw the cab driver smiling at me in the rearview mirror. I looked around to find that we were right outside the entrance to my condo complex.

Invite him in! Invite him in!

You invite him in and I will cut off the oxygen to your brain. Just thank him and get out.

"Thank you for a wonderful evening, Marcos," I said, trying to fix my hair with my fingers.

"It was my pleasure, to be sure. I look forward to working even more closely with you in the very near future," he said with all the sexual innuendo hanging out there for the cab driver to hear.

I grabbed my satchel and climbed out of the cab.

Wave good-bye. Wave good-bye.

Just get inside the gate.

After I unlocked the gate, I turned and waved good-bye. Marcos had rolled down the window and leaning out of the car, blew me a kiss.

"Until next time," he shouted.

What have you done!

❦   ❦   ❦

Even though I hadn't gone to bed until two, I was wide awake by six, waiting for a decent hour to call Marta. By seven-thirty, I had dusted the house, changed the sheets on my bed, unloaded the dishwasher, paid all my bills and even balanced my checkbook. I couldn't think of another thing to do, so I called Marta. When she answered the phone, I didn't give her a chance to look at the clock or even protest.

"I'm coming over. Get up and unlock your door," I said and hung up.

Three minutes later I was at her front door. When I came in she was still in her flannel PJs with the pink clouds, curled up in the fetal position on the couch.

"Coffeeeeeee. I need coffee," she whined.

"You are not going to believe what happened to me last night," I began as I walked to the kitchen to start a pot of coffee.

That peaked her interest enough to get her into the kitchen—that or the smell of coffee brewing. She plopped down on the barstool and cupped her chin in her hands.

"This had better be good," she cautioned. "I was up late last night and was not planning on getting out of bed until after ten at the earliest.

"I met this guy, this absolutely dreamy guy," I gushed just like a teenager.

"Wait a minute," she said, all confused. "I thought you were going out with Bryan last night. How could you meet a guy?"

"I had a business meeting so I had to cancel with Bryan and then the business meeting turned into something else."

Now she was wide awake. So I described the entire evening from start to finish, including all the sexy details in the cab.

"You can close your mouth now," I said with a smile.

Wow. Marta was actually speechless. And then the coffee kicked in and Marta was off and running—running at the mouth, that is.

"Are you out of your mind? A business client? That's a huge no-no. And what about Bryan? I thought you guys were 'seeing' each other. What about him? And what do you really know about this guy? He could be a Don Juan type or maybe he just wants to get you to redo the plans for free. A little whoopee, a little free work—everyone is happy. Everyone but *you*."

"Geez. I thought you'd be happy. Thought you would think it was great," I said, surprised by her reaction. "This guy is gorgeous. And at dinner, when he was holding my hands and looking deeply into my eyes, I got the Zing! Not the lowercase zing, but the big capital 'Z,' Zing."

"Are you sure it vasn't za vine zat vuz giving you za Zing," she said doing a poor imitation of Freud.

"Maybe. I don't know. But I certainly want to find out."

"And what about Bryan? Sweet, perfect Bryan. What are you going to tell him?"

"We are only dating, you know. Nothing has been said about being exclusive or taking it to the next level. Do you see a ring on this finger? I asked, showing her my bare left hand. "So why do I have to tell him anything? It's not like I'm going to sleep with Marcos any time soon."

"Uh-huh," Marta said.

"I'd just like to date him, see what he's all about. Compare him to the List."

"Very interesting that you should bring up the List. You went further with this Marcos fellow in one night than you have with Bryan in two months. You know what I think?"

"I have no idea, but I'm sure you are going to tell me."

"I think," Marta started again. "You are letting your happy place determine your happiness."

"What?"

"You are gushing all over this guy just because he's good-looking..."

"Gorgeous," I interrupted.

"Fine. Gorgeous. And he gave you a physical rush. But you really don't know the slightest thing about him, do you?"

"I know he's rich!"

"Was that on your List, a rich guy?"

"No," I said hanging my head a little. "But," I said hopefully, "He was a perfect gentleman, brought me home in a cab and didn't even try to talk his way in."

"So the guy knows where you live?"

"Oh yeah, right," I said sounding only a bit worried. "It'll be fine. He's a client. I can track him down easily enough if he tries anything funny."

"I've seen you like this before, you know. It was when you first met Bobby. Remember Bobby? The creep who swept you off your feet and then dumped you without a word of explanation. Remember him?"

"Of course I remember Bobby. But Marcos is not Bobby."

"How do you know?"

"I guess I don't," I said, sounding deflated. "You know, this was supposed to be a happy morning, and now I'm all bummed. Thanks."

"Look. I'm not trying to spoil your good time, it's just I've seen you in this place before. The Zing you felt, is just a lowercase zing. Trust me. And the List…the whole point was to help you to avoid falling into this trap again. You were doing so well with Bryan, I'd really hate to see you blow it over some Rico Suave-type."

"You're right, I won't see him again," I sighed. "Finish your coffee. We have to go."

"Where are we going?"

"You have to drive me back to the restaurant to pick up my truck."

"Great. You wake me up and now you're making me actually get dressed, too. It's a good thing you are my best friend."

One hour later we were pulling into the parking garage where my truck was parked. Marta was waiting for me to get in the car before pulling away when I noticed something wasn't quite right. As I got closer to my truck, I could see something red in the driver's seat. Then I screamed, more of a squeal of delight actually, which caused Marta to put her car in park, jump out, and rush over. When I opened the truck door, the aroma of roses poured out over us. The entire cab of the truck was filled with vases of red roses. I reached inside and pulled the little card off of the bouquet in the driver's seat and read it out loud for Marta.

"Thank you for a most spectacular evening. From the moment you walked into the restaurant until the moment you left the cab, I couldn't breathe, I couldn't think, my heart was on fire. Until our next meeting, Marcos."

Marta looked at my glowing face and said, "Oh shit. This is not good."

CHAPTER 10

The Choice

Moments after Marta and I carried six dozen bouquets of red roses into my house, Bryan called. When he asked when he should come by to pick me up Sunday morning for brunch, I casually suggested we meet in the pier parking lot with our bikes. Looking around at the living room filled with flowers I knew I couldn't let Bryan come to my house. So the plan was to ride along the bike path to a funky little restaurant mid-way between the Santa Monica and Venice Piers.

Bryan loved the idea, and sounded thrilled to be seeing me, which made me feel just awful. A little red wine, a few compliments and a couple of well-placed caresses, and I had reverted to my pre-List self. Marta had done her part Saturday morning to make me feel guilty for how I behaved. She had me convinced that it was just a meaningless slip and Marcos probably wouldn't even remember my name the next morning. The truck full of roses had destroyed that theory. While getting ready to meet Bryan, my mind kept wandering back to some of the more intimate moments from Friday night. I had to get back in control, I thought.

By the time I arrived at the pier, I had rationalized every one of my actions and was ready to face Bryan. He was waiting—leaning casually against his truck, his bike at his side—watching the parade of humanity stream by along the bike path. When he heard my truck pull up, he turned and flashed me the biggest smile, as if my arrival was the high point of his day.

Yes, I really am an ass, I thought. I wanted to slap myself hard, just to knock out the lingering images of kissing Marcos in the cab. As soon as I turned off the engine, he was opening my door, leaning in to kiss me before I even had the keys out of the ignition. Ass, ass, ass, echoed in my head.

"How's my favorite girl?" he asked, taking my hand to help me out of the car.

He swung me around so I was facing the ocean and then he wrapped his arms around my waist and pulled my back up against him. He nuzzled his lips into my neck and said softly, "Isn't the beach the best first thing in the morning?"

I answered with a soft, "Uh huh."

Then, after standing there another minute or so, he turned me around in his arms and kissed me, long and hard. I wanted that kiss to clear away the fog in my head—but it didn't. I almost started to cry—wanting so much for that kiss to mean something. Sensing my mood, Bryan pulled back and examined me at arms length.

"What's the matter? You don't seem yourself."

"I'm fine," I lied. "A little tired, is all."

"You want to skip the bike ride and go straight to the restaurant?"

"No. That's all right. I'm looking forward to the bike ride. Maybe it will wake me up," I said without looking directly at him, and started to take my bike off the rack.

Naturally he helped me and then we were off.

He's so nice.

Can't argue with you there.

She never should have kissed that Marcos.

It was nothing. Just a little fun. It was the wine.

That's no excuse, and you know it.

The salty ocean air did wonders for my spirits even with the twins bickering all the way. By the time we arrived at the restaurant, I had managed to bury my feelings of guilt and was determined to enjoy my morning with Bryan. The conversation was fun and lively, until Bryan asked how my "business meeting" had gone. I tried to side-step the issue with a disinterested "fine," but Bryan—always interested in my life—wanted details. The guilt came bubbling up again like a backed up sewer line. Being a terrible liar, I opted for a partial truth.

"The evening didn't go as well as I had hoped," I started.

"How so?"

"My client showed up with a red rose."

"Really. That must have been awkward."

"It was. I was there for a meeting and this guy was acting like it was a date," I said, trying to sound annoyed.

Bryan leaned forward in his seat—a sausage stuck on the end of his fork suspended mid-way to his mouth.

"Like how was he acting," Bryan wanted to know.

"He kept trying to pay for things and did all the ordering and all the talking. It was very frustrating," I said honestly.

"So did you let him pay?" he asked, the sausage still hanging in the air, no closer to his mouth.

"Turns out his brother owns the restaurant so neither of us ended up paying—stale mate," I said with a weak laugh.

"Did you go out afterwards?"

I didn't like the direction the conversation was heading. I felt like I was being grilled and I didn't like it. After all, Bryan and I were just dating. We still hadn't even slept together, so as far as I was concerned, he had no claims on me or I on him. I decided to put an end to the conversation.

"Actually, I was a little tipsy and couldn't drive home. He called me a cab and that was that," I said, taking a bite of toast before continuing. "Marta drove me back to the restaurant Saturday morning to pick up my truck. I just hope we still have the account after the way I treated him. So, how was your night out with the boys? What did you end up doing?"

I continued to eat my breakfast, drinking some orange juice and spreading jelly on a piece of toast I never ate—anything to not have to look at him. When I finally looked up, the sausage had made it to his mouth. I looked at him as if to say, well? Finally he began to tell me about his Saturday night and I breathed a sigh of relief. The subject was finally closed.

It had been a full week since my "relapse," as Marta called it, when the packages started arriving. I came home from work to find a brown paper bundle with ten colorful stamps from Spain in the upper right-hand corner, and my name and address beautifully hand-written across the middle. I wish I could say I wasn't excited, but I was thrilled. I couldn't get into the house quickly enough. I ripped off the paper and opened the plain white box inside to reveal a stunning black silk shawl.

I'm not really a big shawl fan, but it *was* beautiful and it *did* come all the way from Spain. The white card inside read, "The beauty of this shawl will be enhanced when worn by you. I count the days, the hours, the minutes, until I see you again. Marcos"

The guy could write, I thought. He had exquisite penmanship—all loopy and curly, and somehow sexy. That was when my resolve to never see him again began to slip away. Each day, something new would be waiting for me when I came home—a book of poems by Pablo Neruda, a card filled with rose petals, a small wooden box with sand and sea shells from a beach near Barcelona. I got so that by four in the afternoon I couldn't stand to be at my desk another minute. All I wanted to do was rush home to see what was waiting for me.

One day, there was nothing in my mailbox or sitting in the planter outside my door. I was actually a bit pissed. That's it? I thought. But then the next day there were two gifts—a small package containing a silver anklet and an ornate card with gold gilded lettering. In his last letter, he practically begged me to pick him up at the airport saying, "If I don't see your smiling face when I step off the plane, I will not feel I am truly home." After the roses, postcards, letters and gifts, how could I refuse? Marta had insisted on coming with me on the pretext of wanting to meet my new heartthrob. But I suspected it was to put a damper on any extended welcome kisses.

When Marcos emerged from the jet way, he was wearing a dark gray Italian suit with a black Nehru-collared shirt. His jet black hair was perfect, his dark brown eyes searched the crowd for me, and in his hand he held two dozen red roses that contrasted perfectly with his dark countenance. Marta had thought it would be funny to pull a little joke on him, so while I hid in the gift shop across the way, she stood at the entrance to the jet way holding a sign that read "Arlando" as if she was from a car service. The look on his face when he saw Marta and the sign was first confused, then disappointed. The red roses dropped to his side as he walked over to Marta. I felt instantly guilty for disappointing him so.

"I am sorry, but I didn't order a car service Miss," he said, stilling looking around for me.

"Well, one was ordered for you, Mr. Arlando, so please come with me," Marta said, acting all nonchalant. "I hope you don't mind, but we need to duck into the gift shop to get something first."

"I'll wait right here, then," he said, still looking around as if in hopes I was just running late.

"No, I think it would be better if you came with me. I may need your help carrying my purchases," she coaxed, trying to get him to come into the gift shop so I could surprise him.

"Look, Miss," he said, never really looking at her, but still searching the terminal for me. "You run along and get whatever it is you need, but you'll have to carry it yourself. My hands are full and I have luggage to get."

I was watching from just inside the gift shop as our plan unraveled. I could tell by the look on Marta's face that she was getting annoyed, and that Marcos was still anxiously looking for me. This was mean, I thought. I was just about to come out of hiding when Marta gave me a hand signal to stay put.

"Now look here, Sir," Marta said, finally getting his full attention. "She's not coming. She sent me to get you and she wants you to help me pick up this 'something' in the gift shop. So get your fancy ass in there before I have to drag you along."

"You can't talk to me like that. I'll have your license," he snarled under his breath.

"You'll have more than my license," Marta snarled right back, making a small fist with her right hand, "if you don't get into that gift shop right now!"

From my position I could see the situation was going sour fast. Marta had both her hands on her hips and Marcos had crossed his arms smashing the roses in the process. People were making wide circles around the two as they both stood their ground. I decided to intervene before someone got hurt and came out from my hiding place. The moment Marcos saw me, his entire disposition changed. With roses extended, he practically knocked Marta over as he rushed to greet me. He bent over and wrapped his arms around my hips and lifted me into the air, spinning me around in a slow-moving circle. Finally, he set me down and kissed me hard and long. When we pulled apart he gave me the roses and took my hand to leave.

"I missed you so much, Samantha," he said, pulling me toward baggage claim.

"Wait," I said pulling in the opposite direction. "Marta is with me. We were just trying to play a little joke on you—we thought it would be fun."

"Marta, your best friend? Where?" he asked.

"Right behind you, Rico. Your friendly neighborhood car service driver, at your command," she said with a smile that I knew was more like a death ray.

"You? You are Marta?" he asked. "Oh, dear. We have gotten off on the wrong foot then, haven't we?"

"You could say that," Marta said, still not softening.

"Let us start again," he said, pulling a rose from my bouquet and handing it to Marta. "Hello, I am Marcos Arlando. I am so very pleased to finally meet the very best friend of my beautiful Samantha. She has told me so much about you."

"Charmed, I'm sure," Marta said in her best imitation of a Brooklyn accent, giving the rose a good long whiff. "Shall we go? I'm sure your luggage is waiting for you."

Marta led the way, with Marcos and I trailing behind, hand in hand. When we got to the car, Marta jumped into the driver's seat, forcing Marcos and I to separate—me in the front seat, Marcos in the back. I turned around in my seat so I could see Marcos and carry on a conversation. He went on and on about how much he missed me and how Spain wasn't the same without me, and how next time I must go with him. When he got really mushy, Marta stuck her finger down her throat like she was going to vomit, but other than that, she behaved herself.

❦ ❦ ❦

Once Marcos was back in town, he called me every day at work, wanting to know when he could take me out again. Against the advice of Marta and Ms. Goodie, I finally agreed to meet him for dinner. Bryan was out of town on his annual Las Vegas sojourn, so having a simple dinner didn't seem too risky.

Marcos picked me up at four in the afternoon, explaining the restaurant was a bit of a trek. When we pulled into the parking lot of the Santa Monica Municipal Airport, I thought we were going to The Flying Dutchman, a steak house near the airport. When he led me out onto the tarmac, I began to protest.

"Hey. I thought we were going to dinner."

"Oh, we are. We are flying over to Catalina. I have a reservation at my favorite spot in Avalon."

"You're joking."

He wasn't joking. Marcos had chartered a helicopter to fly us over Los Angeles to see the city lights then to Catalina and back—just for dinner. This was way above and beyond any date I'd ever been on. The twins were having a heyday—arguing all the way over to Catalina about whether or not this was a good idea. Once in Avalon, seated at an outdoor restaurant a stone's throw from the gentle lapping of the water, drinking good red wine and watching the boats bob gently up and down with the tide, even Goodie began to relax and enjoy the evening. You had to hand it to the guy—he knew how to wow a woman. When I got back, I have to admit I was in la la land—a little swept away with it all. The first thing I did, of course, was call Marta.

Marta's interpretation of the date was harsh—he's working way too hard and too fast to try and impress you—he only wants to get into your pants. Marta was relentless in her pursuit to find fault with Marcos. She told me how he had treated her at the airport when he had thought she was just some lowly car service driver. Rich or not, you shouldn't treat people that way, she said. She would always ask how Bryan was doing. Had I seen Bryan lately? How was my date with Bryan? She was driving me crazy. She insisted I pull out the List and do a reality check.

"That's what the List is for, isn't it? To make sure you stick to the plan and *not* be swept off your feet by some pretty boy with big bucks," she reminded me more than once.

Bryan and I talked about once a week and we went out on a few more adventures—horseback riding in Malibu and a hike in the Santa Monica mountains. He even came to a couple of my softball games and cheered me on, as I hobbled to first base in my brace. He got along really well with both my brothers and Bridget, although sometimes I felt like they were all keeping some big secret from me. Once, when I walked up to them, the conversation suddenly died and everyone stood there smiling and looking at me very oddly. When I asked Bryan about it, he just made a joke about my brothers sharing family secrets with him.

I didn't mention to Bryan that I was dating Marcos, and I didn't mention to Marcos that I was dating Bryan. As a matter of fact, the only person who knew I was dating both was Marta and she didn't like it one bit. Marta was convinced that Marcos had something up his sleeve other than his arm. She had this one wacky theory that Marcos was just using me to get a better price on the project I was working on for his company. What nonsense—he was spending more money on dating me than he could possibly hope to save on the project. Then she had another theory that I was just the "flavor of the month" and that next month he would pick another victim, especially if I didn't go to bed with him real soon. That was a possibility; I had to admit. The whole sex thing was definitely becoming an issue. On one hand there was Bryan, a perfect gentleman at all time—even when I wished he wasn't. I really liked him and the number of items he was matching on the list was adding up fast. But on the other hand it was difficult to ignore Marcos's extravagant maneuvers. Marcos was romantic, sexy, exciting. Bryan was fun, relaxed, carefree. I figured as long as I didn't sleep with either of them, I was still okay. I knew that someday I would have to make a choice and stop dating one of them because it was getting increasingly difficult to hold Marcos at bay. He was always kissing my hand, playing with my hair, placing me in romantic settings and making sure there was plenty of wine to drink. Greater, stronger women than I have succumbed to less.

❦   ❦   ❦

Marta was throwing her famous annual Halloween party and I was still undecided on what to wear. Marta thought, since the party was on the 20th—the anniversary of the day I awoke from my coma—that I should come, dressed in hospital clothes. I rejected that idea as too boring. I was torn between a Spanish peasant girl, complete with black shawl, to match Marcos's Zorro, and Little Bo Peep, my sister-in-law's costume from last year. I tried it on, and it fit perfectly. She even had the shepherd staff and three stuffed sheep. I thought it would be a kick to place the sheep strategically around the party and spend the night asking people if they had seen my lost sheep. It sounded like a lot more fun than playing a peasant girl to Marcos's Zorro. Bryan was going to be out of town the weekend of Marta's party, so I decided to invite Marcos.

Of course, Marta loved Little Bo Peep and couldn't stand the peasant idea almost as much as she couldn't stand Marcos. I don't know why, but Marta and Ms. Goodie Two Shoes never liked Marcos. The first time Marta and Marcos met, it was like watching two fighters circling in the ring, each waiting to get in their best shot.

The day of the party I was at Marta's, helping her decorate and prepare food. Marta has thrown a Halloween party for as long as I've known her. The only year she didn't have a party was last year when I was comatose. She said it just didn't seem right to be planning a big party when her best friend was lying in the hospital. As it turned out, I came out of the coma right before Halloween, but by then it was too late to put something together.

By the time we were finished, Marta's condo had all the trappings of a first-class haunted house. We had pulled and stretched thirty-five bags of fake spider webs over every piece of furniture and every lamp. There were cobwebs hanging from the ceiling; dry ice in the toilet tanks, both upstairs and down, as well as floating in the punch bowl. We filled the downstairs bathtub with "blood" and put a "dead body" face-down in the water. In the upstairs bathroom, we created the character from the movie *Scream*, white mask and all, and had him peeking over the top of the shower stall. There were plastic spiders everywhere, plastic ants frozen into ice cubes and rubber bats hanging from the ceiling fan that flew in a circle when the fan was turned on. Marta replaced every light bulb in the house with either a black light or some other weird-colored light. The kitchen was decorated like Hell, with a sign above the doorway reading "Hell's Kitchen," a little pun for her New York friends. All the kitchen light bulbs were switched to either red or orange. In fact, Marta had been throwing an annual Halloween party for so many years, her collection of Halloween paraphernalia rivals many specialty stores.

At six, I went home to shower, get dressed and gather my lost sheep. Marcos was meeting me at Marta's at nine, but I had promised her I'd come back at seven to help her with her costume, which was an old crone. Since it was easier for me to apply the warts to the back of her neck and hands, I helped her with her make-up, a reversal of roles for us. By eight, the early birds were arriving, followed by both of my brothers, Bridget and the entire softball team, who seemed to show up all at once, giving the impression that "the party" had arrived. Work friends of Marta's, neighbors and a whole group of people who only get together once a year at this party, straggled in between eight-thirty and nine-thirty.

Zorro made his grand entrance around nine-twenty, donning a black cape and mask, already a little drunk. When I came up to greet him with a kiss, he stepped back to look me over.

"Who are you supposed to be?" he asked, looking at my shepherd staff and bonnet. "I thought you were going to be a Spanish peasant girl?"

"Why, I'm Little Bo Peep, and I've lost my sheep, and I don't know where to find them."

At that moment Marta joined us.

"Leave them alone, and they will come home, wagging their tails behind them," she finished. We both burst into laughter, already feeling the two Bloody Marys we had downed earlier.

Zorro pulled up his mask to have a better look at Marta.

"I see you forgot your costume tonight, Marta," Marcos jibed.

"Watch it, gay boy," she snarled, and taking a pinch of glitter from a pouch tied around her wrist, she blew it down the opening in Marcos's silk shirt.

"Hey," Marcos cried, jumping back as if stung. "What was that for?"

"I've put a curse on you," she said, making her voice sound old and crackly. "From now on, only stupid, shallow women with fake breasts will want to date you."

Then she burst into a disturbing witch's cackle and headed for Hell's Kitchen.

"Doesn't sound like much of a curse to me," Marcos shouted after her.

I grabbed Zorro's hand and led him to the bar that was set up in the corner of the living room. One of the Undead was serving up Bloody Marys with bloody doll-head skewers that held a wedge of lime and an olive. I grabbed us two. No love lost between those two, I thought. I just hoped glitter was the only thing Marta threw at Marcos all night.

The party was a huge success, as it always was, and despite having to keep Zorro and the Old Crone separated at all times, I was really enjoying myself. People kept finding my sheep and bringing them to me and then I'd go hide them someplace new. Every once in a while, we would hear a scream coming from the upstairs bathroom as another unsuspecting female discovered the killer watching her from the shower.

At one point, Marta pulled me into a corner of the kitchen.

"Have you seen your friend Zorro?" she asked in such a way that I knew this was going to be one of those "rag on Marcos" moments.

"Not lately. Why?"

"He seems to have found his new flavor for October and it looks like it's vanilla," she said, not even trying to hide her contempt for the guy. "He's sitting awfully close to a very blonde French maid, in a cozy corner of the living room. Take a look."

I walked over to the doorway of the kitchen and popped my head out. Sure enough, there was Marcos and someone I didn't know sitting nice and cozy in one of Marta's overstuffed chairs. They looked like they were enjoying themselves. She laughed at everything he said with a high-pitched twitter that was most annoying and he just lapped it up. When I turned around, Marta was standing right behind me with an "I told you so" smirk on her face.

"Not a word," I warned. "It's a party and he's socializing. Big deal."

"Okay. If you say so." she said, and then swept past me back into the living room to join the crowd.

Even though I acted like it was no big deal, I stayed in the kitchen for about fifteen minutes on the pretense of cleaning up. When I finally worked up enough nerve to leave Hell's Kitchen I walked through the door half expecting to find Marcos and the French maid making out in the corner. But they were gone. As I was searching the crowd for Zorro I spotted someone I hadn't seen before standing near the stairs at the front door. All I could see was his back, but he looked to be dressed like Daniel Day-Lewis from *The Last of the Mohi-*

cans, which immediately sparked my interest. He was wearing calf-high leather moccasins; fawn skin-looking breeches; an off-white, long-sleeve shirt, with an authentic-looking long rifle slung across his back. He had thick, long, dark hair that reached to his mid-back, and he was talking with Bridget, making her laugh hysterically. I grabbed Marta as she was walking past and dragged her back into the kitchen.

"Who's that?" I asked, pointing toward the stairs.

Marta followed my finger and turned to me and smiled.

"Oh, him. He's an old friend of mine from college," she said casually.

"Do I know him?" I asked, having met most of Marta's friends before.

"I don't think so. This is the first time he's made it to one of my parties. Come on. I'll introduce you," she said, taking my hand and leading me through the crowd.

Marcos saw us coming and tried to intercept us, but Marta formed her hand into a claw and gave him an evil snarl to ward him off as she pulled me quickly past him.

We stopped directly behind the man. Marta tapped him on the shoulder as she said,"Samantha, I'd like you to meet a good friend of mine…"

Before she could finish, the man turned around. It was Bryan.

"Bryan," I gasped, totally caught off guard. "I thought you were going to be out of town."

I had never seen Bryan with his hair out of its ponytail. It totally changed his appearance—he looked absolutely yummy. The mountain man clothing made him look as though he had just stepped out of my favorite movie. My knees suddenly felt like rubber, and I had to lean on my shepherd staff for support. His long hair framed his smile that widened when he saw it was me.

"Well, if it isn't Little Bo Peep? Marta told me you were having a problem with lost sheep, so I canceled my plans to be here. Besides…I wanted to give you these in person this time," he said, presenting me with a bouquet of flowers—tuberoses and white tulips. "Happy Anniversary, Sam. I'm really glad you decided to wake up last year, or I never would have gotten to know you."

The rich, tropical fragrance of the flowers brought me instantly back to my hospital room, where I could vividly recall the vase of tuberoses and tulips on the table.

"It was you?" I asked, still in a state of shock. "You were the one who gave me those flowers at the hospital? But how could that be? You didn't even know me then."

"Yes, I did," he answered, his eyes never leaving mine.

I looked at Bryan, then at Bridget, who had a big, stupid grin on her face and was nodding her head yes. I looked at Marta, but she seemed as stunned as I was by this news.

"I know this is going to sound trite, but I fell in love with you, Sam, the moment I saw you lying in that bed."

Did he say love? Suddenly I needed to get some fresh air and headed for the door, clutching the flowers to my chest. Bryan caught up to me in the garden area in front of Marta's condo where I was trying to remember how to breathe.

"You know I work at the hospital, right?"

I nodded as if in a trance.

"I happened to be making my rounds the night they brought you in. Even in sleep, there was something about you that instantly touched me. The next day, I requested to be your physical therapist. It was my job to bend and unbend your arms, rotate your wrists and ankles, bend your knees, and roll you from side to side every day. You were a feisty one, even in a coma—sometimes kicking me, or saying stuff I couldn't understand. That's why I figured you were going to come out of it in such a short time. You were so full of spunk. I loved that about you, that even in a coma, you were so full of life."

I sat down on the brick planter and took a deep breath. My inner voices were both trying to speak at the same time, which was making the moment seem even more unreal.

See, I told you he's The One.

But what about Marcos?

Marcos is a nobody. Bryan's The One.

"It seems psycho, I know—love at first sight," he said, almost apologetic.

There was that word again, I thought.

"And that's why I've tried to take our relationship so slowly. I wanted to give you enough time to get to know me like I already knew you. You know, catch up."

When I still didn't respond, he rushed on.

"During the three months you were under, I spent a lot of time with your family, your Dad and your Mom, your brothers, even Bridget. You had such a terrific family who so obviously loved you that I knew you must be an incredible person. One time, near the end, I tried the Sleeping Beauty thing, you know, the kiss? It was just past eleven one night and it was between shifts. I was just about to go home when I stopped by your room for one more look at you, and that's when the thought hit me. Wouldn't it be magical if I kissed her and she woke up? So I stood at your bedside and held your hand, like I did each night, and then I bent down and kissed you softly on the lips, just like this."

Then he bent over, cupped my face in his hands and ever so softly, pressed his lips to mine.

"But, of course, it didn't work," he said, standing up again and looking very vulnerable.

"I wouldn't say that," I said, standing slowly. "I woke up, didn't I? Maybe not right that second, but I did wake up. Why don't you try it again?"

That was all the encouragement he needed. Bryan pulled me in close by the waist and looked deeply into my eyes. In a coarse whisper he breathed out the words, "I love you, Samantha. I have always loved you." Then he pulled me in even closer and gently kissed my lips, waiting for my response. And that's when it happened, the Zing. Not the lowercase variety, not the little zing of physical longing, but this huge overwhelming feeling that I was melting into this other person. Suddenly, it was even more difficult to breathe, and I felt weak with happiness. I returned his gentle kiss with one of my own, before pulling back to take him in again.

Bryan had been transformed before my eyes. Whatever defenses he had been using to mask his feelings before were now completely down. What I saw in his face was his love and passion for me. I could see it in his eyes as they burned into mine. I could feel it in the heat of his hard chest and the tautness of his thighs as they pressed against me. I could hear it in the sound of his ragged breath and in the tremble of his hands as he touched my face. And all of it awoke in me a flood of emotion, passion and longing that I'd never felt before for any man. Oh my God, I thought. He *is* The One. The thought was like a lightning bolt—quite overwhelming. I pressed myself into him, and this time, our kiss was not a gentle pressing together of flesh, but a powerful coming together of two souls, an explosion of passion and a promise of fulfillment to come. When we finally pulled apart, we were both breathing hard and our faces were flushed.

"You don't know how long I have dreamed of this moment," Bryan whispered in my ear. "That kiss was even more amazing than I imagined."

My heart was racing, and his breath on my ear was sending waves of sensation down my spine. I wanted to kiss him again and again.

"We should go," I suggested, vivid images of both of us lying naked filling my mind.

I could see Marta and Bridget watching from the open door and didn't want to be the evening's entertainment.

"Where?" was all he wanted to know.

"My place. Let me tell Marta and Bridget I'm leaving," I said, and before Bryan could stop me, I was heading back to the house.

Marta and Bridget had ducked back inside the moment they saw that I'd spotted them spying. I found the two of them chatting casually by the stairs.

"Marta, I'm leaving. I'll be back tomorrow morning to help you clean up," I said, and started back toward the door without further explanation, figuring they knew darn well why I was leaving.

The next thing I knew, I was being spun around and pulled back inside.

"Hey! Where have you been? I've been looking all over for you," questioned Marcos.

Oh, shit.

We shouldn't have come back in. I knew this was going to happen.

Lie and leave, lie and leave.

"I needed some fresh air, so I stepped outside. Now I have to run home and get something. I'll be back in a minute," I lied, not very convincingly.

"I'll come with you."

Suddenly, I was being pushed outside—a drunken Marcos right behind me—until we came face-to-face with Bryan.

"Samantha, who's this?" Bryan asked, sounding surprised. "I thought we were leaving."

'Leaving?" questioned Marcos. "Sam's not going anywhere, especially not with you, Indian Boy."

"Who is this asshole?" Bryan wanted to know, his voice rising a couple of decibels, changing from surprised to pissed.

Before I could answer, Marcos pushed past me until he was standing directly in front of Bryan. The negative energy filling the void between the two men was palpable.

"This asshole," Marcos replied, matching Bryan's tone, "is Sam's date. Any woman who comes to a party with Marcos, leaves the party with Marcos."

Bryan stepped around Marcos to face me.

"Is this true? Did you come with this jerk?"

Deny, deny, deny!!!

She can't. Just say yes and explain later. You've done nothing wrong.

Lie, it's the only way.

The truth comes out eventually—don't lie.

Fudge, then. A half-truth will work here.

The dialogue in my head was making me dizzy. The only thing I could think of to say was a feeble, "Well, sort of…"

Bryan took a step back, stunned.

"Satisfied?" asked Marco, placing his hand on Bryan's shoulder to move him out of the way.

I'll never forget what happened next. Like a scene from a *Kung Fu* movie, Bryan grabbed Marcos's hand, did some kind of turning maneuver and the next thing I knew, Marcos was flat on his back—the wind knocked out of him.

Wow!

Cool!

I'm impressed.

Me, too.

"Samantha."

Bryan was standing directly in front of me. His eyes were locked on mine. Even in the dim light, I could make out the intensity of his gaze and it both frightened and excited me.

"I'm only going to ask you this once. Are you coming with me or staying with him?"

"I'm coming with you," I said, without a moment's hesitation.

"Good," he said, and grabbed me by the hand to leave.

Both Bryan and I saw him at the same time—Marcos back on his feet, arm cocked back to deliver a punch to Bryan's face. I screamed. Because I was holding his right hand, Bryan had only his left to deflect the punch. He managed to avoid getting hit in the face but the shot struck him hard enough in the shoulder to knock us both backwards. Instantly, Bryan released my hand and prepared for the second punch that was already on the way.

Marcos was purple with rage. He looked like a demon, with his Zorro cape billowing behind him, as he swung again at Bryan. In comparison, Bryan was calm as he waited for the attack. Everything he did was in defense. I found myself growing calm as well, as it became obvious that Bryan was in complete control of the situation. My scream had attracted Will, Bridget, Marta and a few others from the party, outside. We all just stood around and watched as Bryan calmly dodged and deflected everything Marcos threw at him. It was the strangest thing to watch.

Frustrated, Marcos let out a cry and charged at Bryan, meaning to knock him to the ground. Bryan dropped into what looked like a football stance—one hand on the ground, feet spread wide, shoulders down, head up. The sound of the two bodies colliding made the small crowd wince and groan.

Marcos went flying, for the second time that night, and landed with a sickening thud on his back. No one moved. We all just waited to see if Marcos was going to get up. He tried, but then immediately gave up and sank back into the wet grass. Suddenly the big-breasted blonde, dressed like a French maid, pushed past us. She knelt at his side and immediately started playing the part of nurse maid. Marta and Bridget gave me looks as if to say, "interesting" as we all watched Marcos lap up the attention like a piglet suckling on a tit. Will walked over to Bryan who was barely breathing hard.

"Nice tackle, Bro," he said, slapping him on the back.

"Thanks. That last maneuver was courtesy of the UCLA punt return team. That asshole probably went to SC."

Will laughed. "Probably."

Bryan slowly walked over to me and grabbed my hand again.

"Let's go." he said. "I think the French maid can clean up the rest of this mess for us."

That was the only thing he said all the way to my condo.

CHAPTER 11

The One

I must have said, "I'm so sorry" at least a dozen times before we reached my condo. And while Bryan didn't say a word, the twins were arguing so much it was giving me a headache.

We've blown it now. He's pissed. He's never going to forgive us.

Sure he will. He said, "I love you." That has to mean something.

I hope it means he wants to make love. Watching him handle Marcos like that really turned me on.

How can you think of sex at a time like this?

I don't know. But I'm terribly horny. Between the fight, his costume and that incredible kiss, I'm ready to rip off his clothes right now.

You are incorrigible. I think we should talk first.

He doesn't seem to be saying much—she says sorry and he says nothing.

By the time we were at my door, I was in tears. I unlocked the door and went straight to the bathroom to wash my face and regroup. I filled the sink with water for the tuberoses and tulips. I took off the silly Bo Peep hat, blew my nose, washed my face and tentatively opened the door. The condo was dark except for the glow of the porch light coming in the living room window. I didn't see Bryan until my eyes adjusted to the dim light. He was waiting for me in Marta's corner of the couch—his head tilted back, his arms crossed at his waist. I went around the couch and sat cross-legged in my corner, facing him, waiting for him to speak. My head was still aching, but the twins were finally silent. After an agonizing minute, I broke the silence.

"We need to talk."

"Yes, we do. Why don't you start by explaining who Marcos is, and why he was your 'date' tonight?"

He didn't sound angry, only tired—that was good. But he also didn't move or look at me, which was bad. I decided to start at the beginning. Once I got started it all came pouring out of me—how he was the client I had dinner with that night; how he filled my truck with roses, sent me expensive gifts from Spain. I even told him about our one date to Catalina. I told him practically everything.

"So you are into rich guys, is that it?"

"No."

"So what was it?"

"I was confused," I stalled.

"What was so confusing? You were dating me. I wasn't confused. I wasn't dating other people. Why were you?"

"I think that was the problem—we were 'just dating.' Don't get me wrong. Our dates were wonderful, fun adventures, but it didn't seem like you wanted to go any further than that or move to the next level. I didn't know what you were thinking. You never told me how you felt—until tonight. So I assumed we were 'just dating,' which made it okay in my book, to date other people as well."

That made him sit up and turn to face me. I could only see the silhouette of his head against the light coming in through the window, his long hair hiding the details of his face. When he spoke it was as if his words were coming out of the darkness. It was eerie and made it hard to know what he was feeling.

"There were others as well? In addition to Marcos?" the black outline of Bryan asked.

"No. Just Marcos and we only went on that one date."

I couldn't stand not seeing his face, so I reached over and turned on the antique table lamp sitting on the end table next to me. Bryan squinted, and put his hand up to block the light.

"Do we have to have the light on?"

That's when I saw his face. It looked like he had been crying and his left eye was red and swollen. I guess Marcos got one punch in after all.

"Oh shit—your eye," I said, and moved over to him.

I cautiously pulled aside several long strands of hair that were hanging in his face. I accidentally touched a spot that made him wince.

"Sorry. Let me get some ice," I said and started to stand up.

He gently took hold of my arm saying, "I'm fine" but I ignored him and easily pulled away. In the kitchen, as I was getting out the ice trays, I spied a bag of frozen corn hidden behind the ice cream. I grabbed the corn and a dish towel, and headed back into the living room. Setting the corn on the coffee table, I lit two candles and turned off the light, before wrapping the frozen vegetables in the towel and applying it to Bryan's eye.

"Thanks," he said, sounding like a small child.

We sat there in the candle light for a few minutes before he spoke again.

"Answer me one thing—did you sleep with that Spanish bastard."

"Of course not," I said immediately. "I was 'just dating' him, I didn't have a relationship with him or anything."

"Did you have a relationship with me?"

"I didn't know—that was the problem—I just didn't know."

"Do you know now? Now that you know how I feel?"

"Yes, now I know. I'm so sorry I put you through all this," I said, and grasped his hand.

"And just so we are on the same page—we agree that we are in a relationship and we *don't* go out with other people, right?"

"Of course not," I sighed. I was so relieved. It looked like everything was going to be all right between us after all.

He gently pulled my other hand away from his eye. Holding both of my hands in his, he said, "I really do love you, Samantha. I want to take it to the next level, and then the next, and then the next."

"So do I."

Letting go of my hands he cupped my face and pulled me into him. Our mouths found each other and slowly rediscovered that moment in the garden. Long, wet, deep, kisses, passed between us. Eventually we pulled apart long enough to look at each other.

"Samantha, you look so beautiful," was all he said before he started biting my neck.

When his hands reached down and cupped my breasts, a sigh escaped my lips and all I could think of was how much I wanted him to touch me—flesh-to-flesh.

"Help me out of this thing," I managed to gasp, as he sucked hard on my earlobe.

I slowly turned around and presented him with the twenty pearl buttons and the ten-inch zipper that was holding my costume in place. Slowly he undid every button, kissing each area of exposed flesh as it was revealed. With every touch of his lips to my bare back, I sighed. When he got to the skirt zipper I stood up to make it easier. He slowly, deliberately, pulled the zipper the entire length before letting the dress fall to the ground. I stepped out of the circle of fabric that was swimming around my ankles and turned to face him.

He moaned when he saw me in my white panties and no bra, and his reaction made me ache even more for him. I knew the moment he touched me that we would never make it upstairs to my bedroom. He leaned forward and kissed my stomach, over and over, with kisses so soft they were barely there. His hands floated over my back, moving down slowly until he grasped my cheeks. I was leaning into him, running my fingers through his hair, when his hands reached inside my panties and slowly started circling around to the front. I pulled away enough to give him room while he gradually pulled my underwear to the floor. I was completely naked in front of him and didn't feel self-conscious at all.

"Samantha," was all he could say, his voice thick with desire.

I knelt down in front of him and began to loosen the leather laces that were holding the front of his shirt together. While I slowly undressed him, running my hands over his exposed chest, he never stopped caressing me. I pulled off his boots and tossed them toward the front door. I ran my hands up and down his thighs until his moans filled the room, teasing him with a slight brush of his crotch, before unzipping his pants. Eagerly he lifted his hips so I could pull off his pants and I was surprised to find he wasn't wearing underwear. Everything was instantly accessible, so I took full advantage of the situation.

By the orange glow of the porch light coming in through the lace curtain of my living room window, and the two candles I had lit, we explored each other's bodies for what seemed like hours before finally taking our relationship to "the next level."

At two in the morning, I awoke on the floor, aware of his body wrapped around mine and the sound of his gentle breathing in my ear. I was cold and longed for the comfort of my bed, the warmth of my down comforter, and the softness of my pillows. I turned slowly in his arms, pulled aside his long brown hair and kissed him awake—my turn to awaken the Sleeping Beauty.

"Come on," I said softly. "Let's go up to my bed."

"I thought I'd never hear you say that," he sighed.

Naked, we climbed the stairs to my bedroom in the semi-darkness and made sure the first time wasn't just a dream.

❦   ❦   ❦

The next morning, I awoke to Bryan's gentle kiss upon my lips.

"Hey. What do you know? It worked this time," he said softly, as he leaned over and kissed me again. "But this time you look different."

"Different? How so?" I asked, not knowing what he meant.

"I mean different from when you were asleep in the coma. I used to watch your face while I was putting you through your exercises, and thought yours was the most beautiful face I'd ever seen—so calm, so peaceful, so perfect. But now I realize it was missing some important ingredients. It was missing your smile, your zest for life, and your passion—all that great stuff that lies dormant just beneath the surface when you are sleeping. I can see it all right here," he said as he traced the features of my face softly with the tip of his finger. "You have little smile lines right around here," he said touching the areas at the corners of my eyes. "And your mouth curls up into a slight smile, right here, even when you are asleep. If I could see this face every morning for the rest of my life I'd be a happy man."

"So you were my physical therapist for three months?" I asked, trying to sort out the overload of information from the night before.

"That's right. And during that time I got to know your family a little. I even saw Marta a few times in the halls, trying to pick up on some of the younger doctors. Of course, she didn't know who I was, so I don't think she ever really noticed me."

"This is kind of weird and creepy, don't you think?" I asked, imagining myself lying helpless in the hospital with strange men having their way with me.

"I guess it could be considered creepy, even illegal, if I had abused my time with you, but I swear, I was totally professional—except for that one kiss," he said crossing his heart.

"So you becoming my physical therapist when my knee was acting up, that wasn't a coincidence, was it?" I asked, already knowing the answer.

"Well, not really, no. When I found out you were coming in for your knee, I begged Jane to let me take over your case. I told her it was a matter of the heart. True love, I said."

"True love? How did you know it was true love? You didn't even know me, at least not while I was conscious," I teased.

"I just knew."

"I don't get that. And now that you know me, really know me, do you still feel the same? Are you still in love with me?"

"Now more than ever. You are absolutely everything I have ever wanted in a woman. You are The One," he smiled, and kissed me again, on the forehead, on my cheeks, on my neck, on my breasts.

His kisses were so soft and sweet, I felt like I was being tickled by a feather and it made me giggle.

"I just don't get how you can be so sure," I sighed, almost ready to accept the fact that this wonderful man thought I was perfect.

"I have a List," he said, as he was kissing my stomach.

"A List!" I blurted out as I bolted upright, causing his head to be jerked off of my stomach. "Did you really say you have a List? I can't believe you made a List!"

"It's not as bad as it sounds," he said, the sound of panic rising up in his throat. "It's nothing nasty or crude. It was just a list of all the qualities I wanted in the perfect woman, the perfect woman for me, that is. That's how I was so sure you were the one."

"This is absolutely amazing," I said, shaking my head.

"I'm sorry if this is upsetting you, but really, the List just helped me to focus on what's truly important and stopped me from making bad choices based totally on external or fleeting qualities—something I've been totally guilty of for years. I always seemed to pick the wrong women."

"Stop, Bryan, just stop. First of all, I'm not mad," I started to explain.

"You're not?"

"No. And I'll tell you why. I have a List, too."

Now it was Bryan's turn to be amazed.

"No shit! You have a List? How weird is this?" he asked, sitting up as well.

"I know," I agreed.

"Now I'm the one who's freaking out. We both have Lists. This is really bizarre," he said, sinking back into the bed.

I could almost see the wheels turning in his mind, and I knew exactly what he was going to ask me next.

"How many items were on your list?"

Bingo! That was exactly what I wanted to know about his List.

"Sixty-five. How many on yours?"

"Fifty-seven. How many things have you checked off?" he asked.

"Before or after last night?" I answered coyly.

"Well, after last night, of course."

"Let's see. Of the items I could check off, I'd say you are up to sixty out of sixty-five."

"Damn! That's impressive if I do say so myself," he said proudly.

"Okay, enough about you. What about me? How many items have you checked off of your List?"

"After last night," he asked just as coyly.

"But of course."

"Hmmm. Let me see…"

He started counting first on his fingers, and then went to his toes, then started adding figures in the air with his finger.

"By my most recent calculations, I'd say…five," he said with a huge grin.

"Five!" I cried, and pulling the pillow out from behind my back, I hit him in the head.

"Physically abusive, are we? Now you only match four items," he said and rolled off the bed before I could hit him again. So I threw the pillow at him, which gave him ammunition to throw back at me. Unfortunately, he was a much better shot and nailed me a good one, right in the head.

"Fine. Now you're down to fifty-nine."

"Still better than four," he said diving back on the bed and tackling me.

He pinned me under his naked body, stretching my arms above my head firmly but gently, and then he started kissing me all over.

"Actually, as of last night, you were fifty out of fifty-seven," he whispered as he nibbled on my ear. "Want to go for numbers fifty-one and fifty-two?"

"Gee, I wonder what parts of my body and yours that would involve?" I replied.

"Why, you nasty woman," he teased, acting all insulted. "Number fifty-one is 'a woman who will cook breakfast the next morning' and number fifty-two is 'a woman who lets me eat food in bed.'"

"Oh, I can make you breakfast all right, but you will have to get off me first," I said with a wicked smile, as I lightly licked his chin and neck with the tip of my tongue.

"On second thought, numbers fifty-one and fifty-two are not that important," he said as he rolled me on top of him, releasing my hands and finding my mouth once more.

❦   ❦   ❦

It was opening day for the Dodgers, and Bryan had bought seats right behind the Dodger dugout from a season ticket holder he knew at work. It still amazed me every time I thought about how the List had worked—not just for me, but for both of us. The List had even worked for Marta, but in a totally unpredictable way.

The night of the Halloween party turned out to be as revealing for Marta as it was for me. Around two in the morning, most everyone had gone home, everyone but a very drunk Will. Besides being too drunk to drive home, he had offered to stay and help Marta clean up, just like he did every year. Usually, I was there, too. With everything but the decorations put away, Marta and Will collapsed on the couch and had a final nightcap to toast another great party, another great softball season, the anniversary of yours truly coming out of a coma, great friendships and the search for true love. This led Will to ask Marta if she had found her one true love yet, and more questions about the infamous List. Since Will had scored so well on the first few items that day in the dugout, he was dying to know how well he rated on the unabridged version.

After a lot of begging and groveling on Will's part, Marta agreed to go upstairs and retrieve her copy of the List. When Marta stumbled upstairs, she caught a glimpse of herself in the mirror and almost screamed. She had totally forgotten she was still in costume, warts and all. So being a little drunk she completely forgot why she had gone upstairs in the first place and jumped into the shower. After a while, Will began to wonder what had happened to Marta and went upstairs to investigate. Hearing the shower running, Will plopped down on Marta's bed to wait, grabbing a woman's magazine off her nightstand and making himself at home. Ten minutes later, Marta came out of the bathroom wearing nothing but a towel and screamed when she saw "some guy" on her bed. The scream scared the hell out of Will, who jumped off the bed like it was on fire and frantically looked around to see what Marta was screaming at.

"What are you doing up here," Marta wanted to know, calming down once she recognized Will.

"I was waiting for you to get the List, remember?" he said very cautiously.

"That's right," Marta remembered, and walked over to her antique spoon collection where she pulled a neatly folded copy of the List out from behind the rack.

Then, with alcohol still dulling all their alarm bells and whistles, both of them got comfortable on the bed, Marta still in her towel, Will in his costume from the party. Sitting on the bed like two giggly teenage girls at a sleepover, Marta started at item number one and went through the entire List, one trait at a time. Every time she would describe a requirement, Will would say, "Yep, that's me," or "I do that," or "That's so me."

The weird thing was, he wasn't just saying it. It was really true. By the time they finished, they weren't laughing or joking around any more. Out of a total of 58 items on Marta's list that didn't have to do with sex, my brother Will matched every single one of them, except knowing how to cook.

"Damn," said Marta, suddenly serious.

"What does it mean?" asked a now sober Will.

"It means you're almost perfect," Marta smiled, looking at Will a little differently than she had an hour ago.

"I knew that," laughed Will, before he leaned across the bed and kissed her.

When Marta first told me this, I was shocked.

"You kissed my brother? Jesus, Marta!"

"We did more than just kiss," she smiled mischievously.

"Oh, my God, you didn't?"

"We did, and it was great. Your brother's amazing," she said, practically glowing.

"Aughhhh. Stop!" I said covering my ears. "TMI, TMI!"

This was too much information—way too much. This was my brother. There were certain aspects of his life I didn't want to know about, and this was one of them. Now I knew how my brothers had felt about me dating *their* friends. Marta was on cloud 10 and continued to recount the events of the evening.

That night—or actually, it was Sunday morning—they had just kissed and, still being a little drunk, had fallen asleep in each other's arms. But the next morning, with the four pages of the List scattered around them, they woke up, took one look at each other and instantly started kissing again.

At this point, Marta spared me any more gory details and would only say that Will was now checked off on an unbelievable sixty-eight out of sixty-nine items. My brother, go figure.

"He's everything I never knew I wanted in a man. I really think he's The One," she sighed, acting all goofy—over my brother—which was simply too weird. "Can you believe it? He's been around forever, right in front of me all this time. It took the List to open my eyes. Amazing, isn't it?"

What I thought was even more amazing was the fact that Will was totally smitten as well. He even admitted to having a crush on Marta for years, but, "Hey, it was just Marta," so he never did anything about it. Ever since Marta's party, they've been inseparable. It's so strange. I don't know if I've lost a friend or gained a future sister-in-law.

❆   ❆   ❆

It had been six months since Marta's Halloween party and Bryan and I, and Will and Marta were still going strong. That night, Marcos had been nursed back to health by the blonde bimbo—who must have done a great job—because I never heard from him again. He still calls the office to ask about his project but thankfully he never asks for me. I think he is embarrassed. Good thing we had a signed contract for his theater long before all this happened. Marta is now convinced she is a witch because her curse on Marcos apparently came true. We all felt the "magic" of the List was weird enough without adding a witch to the equation.

According to Bryan, there was still one final step in the List methodology of finding your soul mate that we had to complete to seal our fate; we had to retrieve our Lists. I told Marta about this final step, and the next thing I knew, she and Will were renting kayaks to paddle out to the buoy in the bay.

"What, you're not swimming this time?" I asked.

"It's April. The water is way too cold," she explained sheepishly.

"Oh, I see how it is. My brother gets to use a kayak but your best friend had to swim," I said in mock anger.

They both just looked at each other, smiled and shrugged their shoulders before walking away, hand in hand.

You've lost her, you know.

Not really. It's just different now.

Yeah, different. Is different the same as good?

I don't know. I guess we'll find out, won't we?

So now it was time for Bryan and me to retrieve my List. We arrived at Dodger Stadium two hours before game time, bypassing the beer and hot dogs for the first time in my life.

"So now what?" I asked, all nervous and excited.

"Now we recover your List from its hiding spot. I already have mine," he said pulling a piece of foil out of his pocket.

"That's it?" I said looking at the little square of tin.

"Yep, the magic List that brought you to me," he said, carefully unwrapping the foil to reveal two sheets of neatly folded yellow paper.

"Can I see it?" I asked, reaching for the pages, dying to know all fifty-seven items on his List.

"Nope. It's like wishing on a star or blowing out your birthday candles—if you tell the person what's on the List, your wish won't come true," he said, covering the paper again with the foil.

"Where was your sacred spot? You can tell me that, right? You know mine."

"I guess that's fair," he said after thinking it over. "This foil packet was inside of a plastic bag, and the bag was inside a Superman lunch box, and the lunch box was buried next to where I buried my dog when I was a kid."

"That's sweet but sad. Why there?"

"Because one of my List items was that I wanted a woman who could be as good a friend as a lover, someone who would be a companion first and lover second. And that made me think of my dog."

"Your dog was your lover?" I joked, which prompted the man next to Bryan give him a weird look.

"My dog was my companion," he said with emphasis on the word companion for the benefit of the guy next to him.

"You're saying you wanted your dream woman to be a dog? So I'm a dog, am I?"

"Yes. You're my wittle puppy doggie," he said in a cute baby voice. "Sit. Stay. Go fetch your List. Good girl," he said and patted the top of my head.

"Very funny. Fetching the List is not that easy," I said and explained to him exactly where and how Marta and I had planted the thing.

He reached into his pocket and pulled out his wallet, extracting a twenty dollar bill.

"Here," he said, handing me the money. "See that bat boy sitting over there by the fence? Go down there, lean over the rail and tell him what you want him to do. He may just do it because you're so cute, and it's a harmless romantic kind of thing. But if he balks, give him the twenty."

So off I went. After two minutes of discussion, the bat boy headed for the dugout. I turned and gave Bryan the two-thumbs-up signal before following the bat boy along the railing. The kid disappeared into the dugout, and after what seemed like a very long time, he emerged holding the plastic roll with duct tape still stuck to it in several places.

"Is this it?" he asked, holding up the pathetic looking wad of plastic, paper and tape.

Little did he know what powerful magic he held in his hands. I thanked him and ended up giving him the twenty anyway, just for good Karma. The twenty seemed to erase the look of confusion from his face, and he left wearing a bigger smile than mine. I carefully pulled off the duct tape, opened the plastic bag, and pulled out the List. There it was—a list of sixty-five neatly written items, almost all of which were embodied in a man sitting ten rows above me—my 60-item man. I placed the List back into the plastic bag and walked up to where Bryan was now standing, waiting for me.

"I see it was still there," he said in amazement.

"What if it hadn't been there?" I asked.

"That would have meant that the List had been absorbed by the universe to become one with the natural forces that brought us together. But that's why we have to retrieve our Lists, or at least make sure they are gone, because now that we have found each other, I don't want my List, or yours, out in the world summoning anyone else," he explained very seriously.

"How do you know all this shit?" I asked as we began walking up the steps to the next level of the Stadium.

"I don't," he admitted. "I'm just making it up as I go. How am I doing so far?"

"You're amazing. Truly amazing," I said shaking my head, still following him up the stairs. "So where are we going now?"

"To the very top of the Stadium, the nose bleed seats I believe you call them."

"How romantic."

Ten minutes later we were standing at the railing of the highest point in the Stadium. We were so high, I could block the view of the entire infield with one hand stretched out in front of me.

"So now what, Oh Master of Ceremonies?" I asked, turning to face him.

"First, we both remove our Lists from their protective coverings and lay them together face to face."

"Very symbolic," I said appreciatively.

"Then I'll rip them in half, giving you one half and me the other," he said as he tore the Lists in half, handing me one half of the papers. "Now rip up your half into the smallest pieces you can."

"How's this?" I asked, showing him dozens of little squares of yellow and white paper.

"Perfect. Now we throw our Lists out over the railing, letting them co-mingle as they fly out into the universe. Then we will seal our fate with a kiss."

"You *are* good at this," I smiled.

We counted to three, and flung the torn remnants of our hopes and dreams over the railing, where an updraft caught them and sent them swirling back up toward us. The pieces circled our heads like hundreds of yellow and white butterflies before the breeze carried them away over the edge again to gently rain down upon the people below. Bryan pulled me into his arms and pressed his mouth to mine, holding me tightly, as if he was afraid I too would fly away in the breeze.

"That was perfect," I said when he finally released me.

"No, you are perfect," he replied, and kissed me again.

"You really are good at this, aren't you?"

"It's a gift."

And then we looked down over the railing and watched as bits of our Lists became one with the magic that was the game, before sealing our fate with a kiss.

Without Feeling

Excerpted from Ms. Walker Bos's next novel, *Without Feeling*, a contemporary romance.

Bonus Book

The décor of Jessica Singer's second floor office at the public relations firm of McMannon & Fitch was a cross between art deco and modern mess. On the pale, sage-green walls, hung black lacquered frames with selected prints from the covers of 1920s' magazines—Vogue, Harper's Bazaar and the New Yorker. Two wall sconces in deep green glass graced the wall opposite the door, adding a warm glow when they were turned on. There was a huge, black lacquered desk in the middle of the room that was only visible when Jessica was expecting visitors. The rest of the time it was covered with works in progress, reports, sketchpads, and a laptop that did double-duty as a Post It note holder. Stacks of cardboard boxes containing brochures, stationary, annual reports, and other printed materials were grouped together by client with bright pink Post Its containing instructions such as "Take to Warehouse" or "Mail to Client" stuck to the sides of the boxes. Storyboards leaned in layers against three of the four walls surrounding the desk, making the office a foot smaller in three directions. A fluted-back brown leather armchair sat off to one side facing the desk for the occasional visitor.

Arms crossed, all her weight on her right foot, Jessica stood back from a row of easels that held five storyboards for a campaign for O'Brien Boats. Unconsciously she chewed on a long, thin strand of her sandy blonde hair—the only outward sign that she was experiencing stress. Concentrating on the five boards, it took a while before the muffled sounds coming from the vicinity of her desk registered in her brain. Someone was calling her.

"Ms. Singer, your ten o'clock is here."

No response.

"Ms. Singer?"

Snapping out of her trance, she slowly backed up, never taking her eyes off the images spread out before her. Stabbing at what looked like a pile of paper, Jessica hit the intercom button.

"Kim. You'll need to stall them. I haven't decided yet."

"What? I can barely hear you."

At this point, Jessica turned around and pushed papers aside to reveal the phone, and picked up the receiver.

"I'm not quite ready. I need about five more minutes. Take them into conference room B and take orders for coffee, tea, whatever. Just keep them happy and smiling until I get there. Okay?"

"You got it," replied Kim, clicking off before Jessica could say anything else.

Jessica leaned against the edge of her desk and resumed her scrutiny of the five contenders. Checking the wall clock—four minutes left—she went into action. First, she selected three illustrations representing the three different directions the ad campaign could follow. Then, after setting the boards by the door, went to her desk and sat down in the red leather chair, pulled open a side drawer and grabbed a tortoise shell mirror and matching lipstick. Not really a fan of lipstick, she applied a healthy layer of Dusty Rose to her lips and then immediately wiped it all off with a tissue, leaving only a hint of color. Then she grabbed a tube of Chapstick and moistened her lips, glanced at the wall clock—three minutes—before grabbing a small tortoise-handled brush and quickly raking it through her hair.

Looking into the mirror, her deep blue eyes stared back at her and she practiced a quick smile, making sure there was no lipstick on her straight white teeth. Satisfied that she looked presentable, but not overly done up, she threw the matching tortoise set—a gift from her mother—back into the drawer. She grabbed her black knee-length suit jacket and threw it on over her purposefully untucked white cotton shirt as she strode to the door with long strides. She adjusted her knee-length black skirt with both hands as she walked and then scooped up the three storyboards on her way out.

As she approached Kim's desk, she noticed the five red client folders Kim had prepared for the meeting and grabbed them as well. As she approached the conference room, Kim emerged. The clients were all seated with fresh cups of coffee before them.

"Thanks, Kim," said Jessica.

"Go get em, Tigress," Kim said softly, so she wouldn't be heard inside the conference room.

Jessica smiled and made a soft "grrrrrrrrrrr" sound as the two women passed. As she stepped into the room, she flashed a brilliant smile that rose into the corners of her eyes.

"Good morning, gentlemen," was the only thing Kim heard before Jessica closed the door behind her. Forty-five minutes later, the door opened and five smiling men emerged, each clutching a red folder. Jessica came out last with the president of the company Harold O'Brien. Both were engaged in friendly chatter as they walked into the reception area.

"I'll have a contract drawn up this week," Jessica was saying.

"Sounds great. I think this campaign is just what we were looking for—a real winner," Mr. O'Brien said with a smile.

Everyone shook hands in front of the elevator and continued to chat until the doors opened.

"I'll call you next week," Jessica said as they stepped in.

She stood there smiling until the doors closed and then began walking back down the hall to her office. Kim's head came up from her work when she heard Jessica's approach.

"Well?" she asked.

Jessica made tiger claws with her hands and said "Grrrrrrrr, I slayed them."

"Which treatment did they pick, the family, fishing or skiing?"

"The family—it was the first one I showed them. They liked it so much I didn't even show them the rest."

"That makes it easy."

"I think showing the client the final results is always easy," said Jessica as she consciously made herself slow down her breathing. "It's deciding what to show them that makes me nervous."

"Well, congratulations. Simon will be pleased."

"I highly doubt that. Simon is rarely pleased with anything," Jessica said as she made clawing gestures at her boss's closed door, which made Kim laugh softly.

Once back in her office, she removed her jacket and threw it over the back of the guest chair before dropping lightly into her own chair. She opened a lower desk drawer and then tipping her chair back, rested her feet on the open drawer. She glanced at the wall clock and noted the time. She would give herself five full minutes to relax and enjoy her success before moving on to her next project.

She tilted her head back until it rested on the top edge of her chair and closed her eyes. She let her mind drift out of the office to the beach by her home where she pictured herself sitting on a towel on the sand—the sun warming her face. She imagined herself scooping up a handful of sand and letting it slowly slip through her fingers. She could almost hear the laughter of children playing at the water's edge and the cry of the seagulls soaring overhead. She took a deep, cleansing breath and then opened her eyes—four minutes and thirty seconds had passed. Not bad, she thought, only thirty seconds off target. Her goal was to be able to close her eyes, and then open them after exactly five minutes had passed. Just as she pulled her feet off of the drawer and repositioned herself at her desk, Simon Fitch, Jessica's boss, rapped two times with his knuckles on the open door and came in without waiting for an invitation.

"Heard you closed the O'Brien account. Did you get a signed contract?"

"Paperwork is being drawn up this afternoon. We should have a signed contract by the end of the week," Jessica replied, making sure to keep the irritation out of her voice.

"Should have and do have are two different things. Make sure you follow through until the contract is signed," said Simon, in a condescending tone.

As if she didn't know that, she thought. She didn't bother to reply because Simon never waited for a reply. He was already walking toward her door. Then, as an afterthought, he casually called over his shoulder, "Good Job."

Wow, thought Jessica, sarcastically. Those classes in employee relations are finally working. With the people skills of a stone—a stone from the coldest regions of the Arctic—Simon Fitch was a difficult person to work for at best and impossible to work for at worst. In his first year as partner, he went through fifteen administrative assistants in a single eleven-month period. Most of them leaving either in tears or in a rage—none of them giving two weeks notice.

Simon was the number one reason Jessica was considering a career move or at least was moving forward on making her dream of writing fiction a reality. Since the age of ten, Jessica had been writing stories. Twenty-eight years ago her stories tended to be about dragons and unicorns, magic princesses and mysterious wizards. The stories of her childhood eventually evolved into tales of teenage angst and moody poetry. Finally in college, her interest in writing became the focal point of her studies, leading her to a career in public relations.

Now at the mature age of thirty-eight, Jessica longed for the writings of her youth, full of emotion and magic, instead of the plastic hype that made her clients smile and herself nauseous.

About a month ago at a client dinner meeting, the wife of the president of the company they were smooging, Margery Wexler, mentioned a class she was taking through UCLA's extention program. At first Jessica feigned polite interest but when the woman continued on with a glowing report on how interesting the experience was and how she could "attend class" via the Internet at her own convenience, Jessica's mock interest became real. This led to an hour discussion between the two women, during which time, Mr. Wexler tried to interrupt on three separate occassions and every time was schussed by his wife.

At the end of the evening, Jessica and Margery were exchanging e-mail addresses and chattering like old school chums while everyone else stood around with their hands in their pockets.

The next day, Jessica was called into Simon's office and reprimanded for becoming so involved in the conversation with Mrs. Wexler that she totally had ignored the client. That afternoon Margery e-mailed Jessica saying what a wonderful time she had had at dinner. It was the first time she could remember that anyone had really listened to her. She also hoped that Jessica would take action and pursue her dream of writing more than just "boring ad copy."

The following morning, Jessica was called into Simon's office again. What have I done now, she wondered. Without preamble, Simon got right to the point.

"Apparently Mrs. Wexler has more clout than we thought. I just received an e-mail saying we have their orange juice account and if all goes well, the entire line of juice products. This was all on one condition, that you would personally oversee their account."

Jessica was trying hard to suppress her smile and remained focused.

"So go ahead and create a contract and send it out by the end of the week. Any questions?"

No apology for the chewing out the day before. No, "good job." No acknowledgement that Jessica had saved the day. Jessica gracefully left Simon's office without a word, knowing that by not saying a word, a single word, she was saying volumes. Her satisfaction was in knowing that Simon knew that he had been wrong about Mrs. Wexler and that the chewing out of the day before should never have happened. But when she was safely behind her own closed door she vented her anger mouthing the word "asshole" in his direction. Besides landing the Wexler orange juice account, her conversation with Margery Wexler had led her to the UCLA Extension program available online, and the opportunity to pursue her life's ambition of writing publishable fiction. Publishable was the key here. Anyone could write fiction, but actually getting paid to do so was another matter entirely.

Jessica glanced at the clock. She could probably squeeze in one small project before her lunch meeting with the art department. Unlike Simon, Jessica showed her appreciation for a job well done and liked to build good working relations with the people she depended on every day. She especially enjoyed sticking Simon with a hefty lunch bill about every other week. So whenever there was a new project to discuss, Jessica would schedule a lunch "meeting" and take the three illustrators to lunch to go over upcoming projects and concepts. Today was going to be more of a congratulatory lunch for landing the O'Brien deal. Jessica knew it took the creative talent of her illustrators to bring her ideas and concepts to life and never took full credit for her successes.

Grabbing a stack of client folders off the floor next to her desk, she began reviewing the status of each account, making "to do" type notes on Post Its and sticking them to each file folder. After about thirty minutes her pad of stick on notes were depleted. She reached into her top drawer to pull out a new pad but found none. Picking up the phone she dialed her assistant.

"Hey, Kim. Do you have any Post Its up there? I'm completely out."

"I'm sure I do, but let me look." There was a brief pause and then she was back on the line. "I have several unopened packages of really small ones, two packages of the medium square ones, and three packages of the larger rectangles. What do you want?"

"How about one of each to start. I'll come up and get them. I need to move. Could you order me more of all three sizes? You know I can't function without them."

"No problem."

"Great, I'll be right up."

She knew it was odd in this age of computers and Palm Pilots to be so dependent on little yellow pieces of sticky paper, but everyone has their own system, she reasoned, and this was hers.

With a new supply of Post Its, the rest of the morning flew by without a hitch. Lunch with her illustrators ran a little over the allotted hour and since Fitch was even later, there was no one at the office to make a fuss. The afternoon seemed to fly by and for once she left the office at closing time. Most days she didn't care when she got home since there was no one there waiting for her except a rather loud cockatiel named Wilbur.

But tonight, she was excited to get home and it showed in her stride. Her normal twenty minute stroll from the office to her perfect little rent-controlled apartment two miles away was shortened to fifteen minutes as she rushed her steps in anticipation.

Tonight was the first class in her online extension course Creative Writing 235. According to the counselor, this class was a bit different from most, with a video-taped lecture available for viewing twice a week. The first class had been available online since ten that day. There had been more than a few times at lunch when she found herself itching to rush back to the office for a quick preview, but had forced herself to wait. Now she couldn't walk home fast enough.

As she rounded the last corner and headed down the narrow tree-lined street in a quiet residential area of Santa Monica, Jessica had to resist the urge to sprint the last block. After what seemed like an eternity, she was finally at her apartment, keys in hand as she took the steps to her front door two at a time. Entering her apartment like a small tornado, she dropped her satchel and purse the moment her feet crossed the threshold. The crash of leather meeting hardwood startled Wilbur the cockatiel and made him squawk loudly.

"Same to you," she answered as she went directly to her computer, which was set up in a corner of her small living room, and turned it on. While she waited for the computer to do its start-up calisthenics, she kicked off her heels, took off her jacket and tossed it on the small burgundy sofa. Then with a trick she learned at camp, she unbuckled her bra in the back, crossed her arms and reaching her hands up inside her shirt sleeves, grabbed the shoulder straps and pulled them down and out of the sleeves and over her hands. Then, like a clever magician, she grabbed one end of the bra and pulled the entire thing through her left sleeve, tossing it on the couch, all in one fluid movement.

"Ahhh," she sighed in relief, finally free of the cruel cotton restraint.

Then she hurried into her bedroom, plopped onto the bed and pulled off her pantyhose so quickly that she ripped them.

"Shit," she said, examining the giant hole she had caused, before tossing them in the general direction of the white wicker wastebasket.

She quickly unzipped and pulled her skirt off, leaving it on the bed. She grabbed a pair of men's plaid flannel pajama pants off a hook behind the door and tried putting the pants on as she left the room. She found herself hopping on one foot to catch her balance as she made her way back to the living room. Comfortable at last, she made a quick check of the computer and found it was ready for her password. She typed in "jessthemess," a nickname she had had since childhood, and hit enter. With four quick steps she was in the kitchen grabbing a beer from the fridge, a jar of peanut butter from the cupboard, and a wooden spoon from a jar filled with wooden spoons before returning to her computer.

She entered the address of the online extension homepage and waited for the start of her new career to begin. She had pre-registered months ago, so all she had to do was enter her password and up came the introduction page. One more click and the video would begin. She had absolutely no idea what to expect and her hand froze over the mouse, almost afraid to make the final click.

"Here goes," she said out loud, her voice barely loud enough for Wilbur to hear.

But he did hear and squawked encouragingly. Suddenly the image of professor Brant Wilson stared out at her, followed by his voice filling her living room.

"Welcome to Creative Writing 235, or as I like to call it, Writing From Your Heart."

"Well hellooooooo, professor," Jessica purred. "Hey Wilbur, the professor here is a real hottie."

Jessica tipped her chair back and took a swig of her beer. Now this is the way to take a class, she thought, her bare feet on the edge of her desk. For the next hour, Jessica didn't move, except to slowly nibble at a glob of peanut butter on the wooden spoon. The more she listened the more she wanted him to talk. The way he looked directly into the camera made her feel as if he was talking one-on-one, just to her. When he softly chuckled at his own small jokes, it gave her goosebumps up and down her arms. When the lecture was finally finished, Jessica looked at the clock on her computer in surprise. That was an hour? she thought. Then she realized she hadn't even taken notes. Luckily it was only a matter of hitting start again to replay the entire class—a definite advantage over a live classroom experience.

After watching the class for a second time, and this time taking notes, Jessica finally had her first class assignment.

"What I did on my summer vacation," she said out loud. "What summer vacation?" she asked Wilbur, thinking about how she hadn't taken off more than an occasional three-day weekend in four years.

Maybe I should write a fantasy piece on what I *wish* I'd done on my summer vacation, she thought with a wicked smile, picturing herself and professor Wilson lying side-by-side in a hammock on some tropical island paradise.

"Mommy's having nasty thoughts about her teacher, Wilbur. Bad Mommy, bad."

To which Wilbur replied with a long, slow whistle.

"You can say that again."

And he did, which made Jessica burst into laughter.

"You are a silly bird," she said playfully, and went over to his cage to let him out.

Bringing a yellow writing pad, a pen and Wilbur over to the couch, she made herself comfortable and began to think, letting Wilbur run loose. She made several false starts, each time crumpling the paper into a yellow ball and tossing it at a wastebasket near the computer desk. Wilbur found this very exciting and every time she made a toss, he would run back and forth across the top of the couch and whistle.

When she finally made one in the basket she said, "Two points! Wilbur, you are suppose to say, 'two points' when I do that. Come on, say it, two points, two points." But Wilbur just squawked. "Fine. Be that way. See if I ever take you to a Lakers' game."

Finally she had an idea that seemed acceptable and began to write. As she worked, Wilbur hopped onto her shoulder and played with strands of her hair, but even that didn't distract her—she was in the zone. The words were flowing and she couldn't stop. She was smiling as she wrote, a new experience for Jessica, and the words just kept pouring out of her. Wilbur slowly walked down her arm and tried to bite at the moving pen in her hand, but Jessica was so focused she didn't even notice. An hour later she was done with her first draft. Moving to the computer, Wilbur now on her head, she clicked over to her word processing program and began typing. Twenty minutes later, after a few revisions, she was done. She printed out a copy and grabbing another beer from the fridge returned to the couch to read it over one more time, before sending it off to her dreamy professor.

To be placed on an advanced mailing list for this book, please contact the author at christie.mountaincreative@verizon.net

0-595-29239-9